Preternatural Haze:
A Peculiar Short Story
Collection

By
Violette L. Meier

Viori Publishing

Viori Publishing

Decatur, GA

This book is a work of fiction. The characters and events portrayed in his book are products of the author's imagination. Any similarity to real people, living or dead, business establishments, events or locales is coincidental and not intended by the author.

ISBN: 979-8-9886827-2-1

Printed in the United States of America

Cover Designed by Viori Publishing

DEDICATED

…to lovers of the weird. You are my people.

…to my family, friends, and fans. I am so grateful for your support. You are my everything.

…to God. Thank you for this life.

OTHER BOOKS BY VIOLETTE L. MEIER

PROSE

Out of Night: The First Chronicle of Zayashariya

Angel Crush

Son of the Rock
(Sequel to Angel Crush)

Archfiend
(Part 3 of the *Angel Crush* saga)

Ruah the Immortal

Oracles

Tales of a Numinous Nature: A Short Story Collection

Hags, Haints, and Hoodoo: A Supernatural Short Story Collection

POETRY
Violette Ardor: A Volume of Poetry

This Sickness We Call Love: Poems of Love, Lust, & Lamentation

INSPIRATION
Living and Loving Life One Day at a Time

With All My Being

CHILDREN'S BOOKS
I Would Love You

Would You Love Me?

Preternatural Haze: A Peculiar Short Story Collection

By
Violette L. Meier

TABLE OF CONTENTS

A Closer Look into the Garden

In the beginning, God created heaven and the earth.

Ancient writings said that the earth was waste and void and covered in darkness and the spirit of God was hovering over the face of the primordial waters. Somewhere in this formless, flooded, lightless void, there were beings that dwelled with The Divine Spirit. Some called them angels, others called them orishas, Anunnaki, spirits, lwa or loa, the heavenly court, atmospheric beings or avatars, bodhisattvas, or mana. Whatever they were called, they existed almost as long as the being that created them. Maybe they always existed. No one knows, but what is known is that they existed before humankind inhaled and became living souls.

With a big bang, God brought order from chaos. God spoke the universe into existence; created matter and dark matter, galaxies and all that lies within them. God formed the earth and the plants and animals that came to live upon it. A divine spark, pure energy, was deposited into a material body.

All over the earth, out of the dust of the earth, humans were formed two by two. Each couple became the predecessor of every culture and tradition. The most famous of these first couples were Adam and Eve; two exquisite beings -intelligent and in-tuned with the earth, skin dark like the earth that formed them and hair thick and flowery like endless meadows of solidago.

Adam and Eve garnered fame in a garden called Eden, and this is their story.

On the sixth epoch of creation, God and God's ethereal crew formed humanity. Being perfect beings, the divine ones created male and female in their likeness and told them to rule the land and sea. The holy ones blessed them with an insatiable curiosity so they could discover all of creation and someday create for themselves, for being a creator is the ultimate replication of God. God also instilled in their hearts desire, deference so they could be fruitful and fill the earth with others like themselves, and they did.

Everything they would ever need was already inside of them. and God saw that his creation was good. God blessed them, then left them.

Adam and Eve were vegetarians and were offered a garden filled with fruit and vegetables to satisfy their tongues. They were permitted to eat from almost every tree and to delight themselves with the savoriness, the sweetness, the tartness, the sourness produced by the earth. The couple was expressly forbidden from eating from the tree of knowledge of good and evil and the tree of life because the trees held the keys to immortality and universal knowledge. Such power in the hands of the immature would surely lead to death and destruction.

Adam and Eve, blissful and pulsating with contentment, filled their time indulging in food, sensual desires, and exploring their brand-new home. Days and nights blended as they discovered new plants and animals, new flavors, new sensory excitements, new animal songs, and new heavenly wonders like shooting stars cutting through the night sky and eclipses casting shadows on their world. There was never a moment of tedium as they walked their vast garden. The two shared their innermost theories regarding the purpose of their creation.

While investigating the earth, Adam was moved by hands-on discovery and the desire to create things himself. He wanted to know how things worked; how nature replicated; how animals mated; how all living things knew how to exist instinctually.

Eve, on the other hand, was more inspired by why things were. She wanted to know why God decided to make them; why God would place trees before them and forbid them to touch it; why they were made in the likeness of God minus the divinity. She wanted to know The Divine and the inner workings of the spiritual beings that accompanied The Creator.

Together Adam and Eve discussed all that was terrestrial and ethereal, seamlessly sharing their insights and complementing each other so completely that they operated on one accord.

One day as Adam and Eve walked hand in hand down a freshly hewn path, a striking creature stepped out into the opening with a crafty smile on its peculiar face.

Eve's eyes lit up as she admired the serpent's smooth emerald skin and yellow flickering eyes. His serpentine body curled like kinky hair. Robust and long, with short legs covered in iridescent scales freckled with flecks of gold, the serpent was unique and alluring. There was no other animal like it in the garden.

"Hello," the serpent hissed; his words like a song floating from its lipless mouth.

Adam smiled and waved his greeting.

Eve smiled and said hello back to the beautiful beast.

The serpent said, "I have been watching you two for a while and have become intrigued. May I approach?"

Adam nodded.

The serpent closed the distance between itself and the couple in one step, its giant body rolling like a fleshy wave of sparkling scales.

"How are we intriguing?" Adam asked; one of his eyebrows raised. There was something atypical about the creature; nothing like the other animals. For one, it talked. None of the other animals had ever uttered a word. The look in the serpent's eyes also unnerved Adam. Its eyes twinkled like stars. They were intense, nearly unblinking, and quite hypnotizing. Adam quickly looked away.

"I hear your conversations," the serpent hissed. "Your intelligence is divine," it exclaimed. "Did you know that?"

Eve laughed at the serpent's lisp. Its words sounded almost like a whistle.

It hissed with a bit of annoyance.

Eve nodded her response, smiled, and quietly analyzed the serpent's jeweled exterior.

"I've never seen you here before," Eve cooed, her eyes prancing as they walked over every inch of the serpent. The beast's beauty was both appealing and abhorrent.

"Adam," Eve said. "I thought we named all the animals in our garden."

"I thought we did too," Adam replied, trying to avoid the serpent's beguiling eyes.

"You're such a fascinating creature," said Eve as she bit her bottom lip and resisted the impulse to draw closer.

"You have no idea," the serpent hissed under its breath.

"Are you from another garden?" Adam asked. "Maybe the garden in the land of Nod?"

The serpent shook his head from side to side indicating that he was not from another garden.

"What is your purpose?" Eve asked, wanting to run her fingers down its scales. She wanted to know if they were as hard as the sparkling gems that lined the caves on the edge of the garden. She wanted to know if her fingers would cause a tickle and turn its hissing into a bizarre giggle.

"To educate," the serpent hissed, "and your purpose is to learn."

Adam stared at the serpent careful to avoid its eyes. The serpent looked like a giant bejeweled snake with burly legs and enigmatic eyes. Adam had never felt danger before in Eden. Eden was an innocuous paradise. Something foreign was bubbling up in his stomach making his heart thump triple-time and causing his brow to become wet like rain. Something about the serpent made him want to run, but he didn't. The serpent was way too interesting to flee from. Adam wanted to know more about it.

Eve was definitely intrigued. The intelligence of the serpent far surpassed the other animals. It was obvious that the creature knew many things. It carried itself like one of the holy spirits. Power exuded from its eyes. A preternatural aura pulsated from it. Eve wanted to know what it knew. She wanted to open the creature's head and see what mysteries resided there. She felt it would be nice to have another perspective outside of Adam's and God's.

The serpent discerned Eve's curiosity and a shrewd smile spread across his partially scaled face.

"May I walk with you two?" the serpent asked, careful to position itself on the opposite side of Eve.

"Sure," Eve invited after receiving a slow and hesitant nod from Adam.

Adam interlocked his fingers with Eve's and the threesome started down the path together. As they walked, they spoke of infinite possibilities. Adam shared his questions about anatomy, the stars, and the cellular makeup of lifeforms. Eve shared her ponderings about God, the spirits that dwelled with God, and the soul that animated her and Adam.

As they walked, the serpent taught them many things.

The serpent taught Adam how to make fire, about the gaseous masses in the heavens, and the microorganisms on earth. It taught Adam how to dig in the earth for metals, rocks, and minerals.

The serpent taught Eve how to manipulate the elements with the power of her words, how to mend with plants. It taught her how to summon earthbound spirits to do her bidding, how to read the stars, and how to pull power from the earth. The serpent showed her how to enhance her beauty by using the color of berries upon her lips and ash on her eyelids.

The serpent taught them unfamiliar techniques of carnal pleasure that made their bodies react in ways their imagination could never have conjured. It taught them how to capture animals and force them into servitude, and how to make objects good for cutting, chopping, and building things.

Adam and Eve were in awe of their newfound abilities. They couldn't wait to expound upon their new knowledge and share with God all they had learned from the serpent, especially the carnal delights that made them feel like divine ones every time they climaxed. The couple decided in their hearts that the serpent must have been one of the many gifts God had left in the garden for them to discover.

"I can't wait to show God all I have learned," Eve exclaimed as she picked plants for her enchanted experiments.

The serpent's face twisted, its scales stacking then smoothing out. Displeasure wrinkled its brow. It couldn't believe that Eve's first thought was to share her knowledge with God although God had not shared knowledge with them. The Tree of Knowledge was in the middle of their garden, and they were forbidden to touch it, yet they didn't feel slighted in the least. Vexed by their loyalty, the serpent hissed under its breath.

Orange and purple colored the sky. The sun was beginning to fade below the horizon. They had walked, talked, and experimented all day long.

"I'm hungry," Adam admitted as he plucked a juicy fruit from a nearby tree.

The serpent's countenance brightened. An idea popped into its brain.

"Follow me," the serpent instructed, its green body catching the moonlight each time it coiled. It amazed Adam and Eve how it seemed to walk and crawl at the same time.

"I know where the sweetest fruit is," said the serpent as its thick body made a path through the garden.

Adam and Eve followed the serpent to the center of the garden, stepping over lush greenery and stooping under low-hanging trees. When they arrived in the center, two unspeakably beautiful trees stood side-by-side upon a carpet of vivid violet flowers. The smell of the tree's fruit overpowered their senses. Saliva ran from the corners of their lips. Thunder erupted within their stomachs. Never had the couple desired something so much in their short lives.

"Those are the best fruit," the serpent pointed its emerald talons. "Enjoy! God said that you can eat from every fruit tree in the garden, and these are the best trees."

"That's not what God said," Eve corrected the serpent.

Adam licked his lips and neared the trees; the scent of the fruit causing his feet to move unconsciously, uncontrollably, unwillingly.

Eve continued, "God said that we can eat from every tree except the tree of knowledge of good and evil. Not only should we not eat the fruit, if we touch it, we will die. We don't want to die!"

The serpent laughed aloud, mouth wide and tongue dancing. It stopped abruptly, its eyes narrowing into a line of fire.

"You won't die if you touch it! God just wants to keep you ignorant because God knows that knowledge is power, and power is deific. If you eat from the tree of knowledge, you will become like the spirits of heaven and you will become omniscient like God. If you eat, your eyes will be opened. Your intellectual blindness will be lifted. So many of your questions will be answered. Think about it. If God really didn't want you to eat it, God wouldn't have put it in the center of the garden. God wouldn't have made it look and smell so delicious. Such a cruel temptation! The fruit is here for the picking!"

Eve's heart leapt at the possibility of gaining true spiritual understanding. She contemplated deeply. Her soul groaned. Why would The Creator want them to be ignorant? Why wouldn't The Creator want them to truly understand the world around them and the intricacies of their minds? Why wouldn't God want them to be like God? After all, they are made in God's image minus God's wisdom knowledge and understanding. That seemed terribly unfair. Frankly, not only was it unfair, but it was also malicious to taunt them with the possibility of enlightenment. Eve's eyes went from almond-shaped to dark slits. Anger filled her from her scalp to her toenails. There was so much she wanted to know and so much she wasn't being told. Why was the serpent wiser than her and Adam? They were supposed to have dominion over the earth, yet that crafty beast knew more than they did!

Eve marched over to the tree of knowledge, her dark brown face scowling. She reached up and encircled the aromatic, fuchsia fruit with her long, thin fingers. The odor was orgasmic. Eve pulled the fruit to her lips; her heart thumping like the drum she made under the serpent's tutelage. Fear entangled her being. God's warning echoed in her mind. She froze.

"What are you waiting for?" the serpent hissed. "Don't be afraid to take what's duly yours. You have the right to know who you are and why you're here and what you're made of and your purpose on this earth!"

Adam looked at his wife. His stomach growling raucously. The fruit called out to him. He could taste the aroma on his tongue.

"Eat it!" the serpent urged on the edge of frenzy; its stout feet stumping the ground crushing violets into slimy bits. "Eat it!"

"What if we die?" Eve whimpered as the hypnotic scent floated into her nostrils. She had seen fruit rot and wondered if darkened decay would be their fate. Would they be insect food? Stinking corpses defiling paradise?

"You are touching it! Are you dead? Didn't God tell you if you touch it you will die?" the serpent hissed; its fiery eyes burning with rage, its tongue shooting out between two dangerously sharp fangs.

Adam backed away and pulled his wife behind him.

"Why are you so invested in this?" she asked the serpent, whose forked tongue was flicking in and out of its mouth like a pointing finger.

"I'm not!" The serpent tried to calm itself to no avail. "I am just trying to help you. You said that you wanted to know more and I, your friend, I'm trying to help you receive what you want."

The serpent was right, Eve thought. It was only trying to help. She looked at the forbidden fruit and inhaled its intoxicating scent. Nothing on earth was so appetizing. She held it to her full, round lips, opened her mouth, and allowed her teeth to cut into its fuchsia skin. Sticky wetness covered Eve's mouth from lips to chin. She cooed. She moaned. She let out an amatory sigh. Never had she tasted anything more delicious, felt anything more gratifying than knowledge.

Adam stood next to her; eyes bulging and lips hungry. She handed him the other half of the fruit and he ate it greedily, savagely, quickly.

Their eyes opened.

For the first time, they noticed the different but unique beauty of their bodies. A burning sensation gathered in both their bellies. They were naked, bare, and oddly ashamed of being uncovered in front of the serpent. It seemed that nudity was an intimate secret that should only be shared between lovers.

The serpent looked at their firm strong bodies and flicked its tongue. The couple fled from the lusting eyes of the serpent and hid themselves. They stitched together loincloths from fig leaves then reappeared, rejoining the serpent beneath the tree of knowledge.

"How do you feel?" the serpent inquired.

"I'm not sure," Eve admitted, still conscientious about the flesh peeking through her fig leaf toga.

Adam said nothing. He was too busy exploring the world around him with new understanding.

The Holy Spirit moved through the garden like a gentle breeze, rustling leaves and whistling through the trees. Divine footsteps drew near the couple.

Panic, shame, and fear reverberated from their bodies. They ran and hid, fearful of the repercussions of their disobedience. Suddenly, the idea of knowing more didn't seem worth betraying the trust of The Creator. Eve silently damned herself. Maybe she should have asked God for wisdom, knowledge, and understanding instead of taking it for herself.

Adam hated himself for silently complying as the serpent seduced him and his wife. Images of hot mouths, wet tongues, slick fingers, hard parts, tight... vomit spilled from his throat like a waterfall falling from a cliff.

"Where are you?" God asked, already seeing them trembling behind a luscious green bush dotted with pale berries.

Adam stood up and bravely approached The Creator. Although Adam had done little to prevent their fall from grace, he stepped bravely to his fate. Eve stood close behind him, and the serpent stood grinning behind Eve.

"W...w...we heard your spirit m...m...move and we hid because of our n...n...nakedness," Adam stuttered.

"Who told you that you were naked?" God asked. "Did you disobey my command and eat the sacred fruit?" God's voice rolled like thunder through the trees.

Sweat began to trickle down their sienna skin and drench the ground beneath their feet.

Adam trembled. Tears fell from his eyes. He swallowed hard as if a giant fruit pit was stuck in his throat.

"The woman that you gave me handed me the taboo fruit and I ate it," he cried while pointing to his wife, his muscular arm quaking from shoulder to fingertip.

Eve's eyes stretched in disbelief. Water began to pool in her eyes as her chest tightened and her breath quickened. Never had she felt such emotion. It made her head swim like the innumerable fish she and her husband named together.

"Adam! How could you say that? You ate as I ate. You listened to the serpent as I listened to the serpent!" Eve cried.

Shame heated Adam's cheeks. The look in his wife's eyes devastated his being. Not only was he a disappointment to God; he was also a disappointment to his soulmate.

"Forgive me," he whispered too low for her to hear.

Eve turned her face from her husband and faced God. Through clenched teeth, she wailed, "The serpent deceived me, and I ate the fruit!" She pointed a trembling finger at the emerald creature that was now grinning from one side of its head to the other.

"You wanted it," the serpent hissed, its eyes burning bright. "Eating was your choice. I didn't force either of you to do anything. Everything that transpired today was your choice. Everything was consensual. Tell the truth. You enjoyed everything, especially the naughty tricks I taught you. Didn't you?"

Eve's countenance fell. A tingling sensation gathered below her navel and spread quickly through her pelvis.

Adam glowered at the serpent and pulled his wife behind him.

"Don't get mad now," the serpent laughed at Adam's glowering face and balled fists. "You enjoyed yourself too!"

"Curse you!" God thundered, his voice vibrating through them like an infinity of chimes, paralyzing the three in fear.

A scream ripped from the serpent's mouth. Its legs crumbled into emerald dust and its brawny body fell upon the earth with a wobbly thump. Its beautiful, jeweled scales melted into slick skin. Its articulate tongue shortened, and its hisses thwarted its ability to articulate. Anger bottled up inside of its' body and transformed into venom. The serpent became nothing more than a snake. A simple but dangerous beast whose progeny would be destined to be an adversary to all humankind. The serpent slithered away as Eve gasped in horror.

"What of me, God?" Eve cried. "Will you make me crawl like the serpent? Will you punish me for wanting to be like you? Are we to be cursed for simply wanting to understand your inscrutable mind?"

"Enough!" God roared. "You could have asked me for what you wanted! I would have given you wisdom generously without finding fault with you asking."

Eve cried aloud, "Forgive me!"

"For your insolence, pain will be your punishment. You will bear children and suffer every time you bring life into the world. You will feel the pain of your betrayal, to know how it feels to have your children thoughtlessly disobey you. Your vanity has condemned you! You will swallow your pride and be weakened by your husband. Your love for him will relinquish you of your power. He will rule over you via brute strength. He will not respect you as his intellectual equal but will force you to quiet your voice and submit to him."

Falling to the ground and screaming to the top of her lungs, Eve begged for God to change her fate. Eve howled and beat her breast.

Dust, tears, and mucus filled her mouth as she lay prostrate before the Lord of Hosts. Her pleading went unanswered. She had damned her daughters to perpetual oppression.

Adam looked to the Lord and inhaled deeply, trying fruitlessly to prepare himself for what was to come.

"Because you happily followed your wife down the road to perdition without even a moment of pause, you will never find rest! You did not speak up when you should have! You did not intervene nor think for yourself! You did not stand up to the serpent as it convinced her to disobey me! You, Adam, willingly disobeyed me too by giving into temptation and obeying the serpent instead of me! For your insolence, you will labor with your hands because you failed to use your mind! You will work with your body and contend for your soul. Life will be a hard burden for you. You will work and never be satisfied with your earnings. You will toil and sweat until the day you die."

Adam cried aloud and fell to the ground alongside his wife. They clung to each other as black clouds darkened the heavens and thunder and lightning ripped through the sky. Hail stung their skin. They shuddered beneath the rage of a seemingly cruel and merciless God.

"Forgive us!" they wailed. "Please."

"Get out!" God thundered.

The wind bent the trees as lightning struck the ground around the distraught couple.

Cherubim with flaming swords descended upon the earth swinging their blades like burning pendulums driving the couple down a dark and jagged path out of the garden. The cherubim stood guard on all sides ensuring that the couple could never return to the only home that they had ever known.

"Forgive us!" the couple wailed as their voices faded beneath the crackling thunder. They walked until the garden was so far behind that the memory of it was like a dream.

The snake slithered to the feet of God. A bright light flashed from its body as it transformed into The Morning Star and rejoined The Host of Heaven.

"Why did you send them away?" The Morning Star asked.

"Because they were daring enough to gain knowledge, if they have would have eaten from the tree of life, they would have become one of us," God replied and ascended into the heavens, vanishing from the earth.

"What's wrong with becoming one of us?" The Morning Star mumbled as it glowered at the fleeing couple. It knew it would see them again and their future children one day because humans, like itself, would always wrestle with the unfair and indecipherable mind of God. The Morning Star knew it would also find itself homeless one day.

People will always crave knowledge and power, and The Morning Star will always be around to help them find it for a price that they will gladly pay no matter how disastrous.

The Beginning...

Obscure Artifacts

"One hundred and six degrees," Celia's cell phone chirped in a robotic feminine voice. Hot sweat ran down her forehead burning her eyes and verifying that the obscenely feverish temperature was true. She adjusted the thin white scarf that draped her thick spirally hair like a bedsheet and continued to walk.

It was Celia's first time in Egypt. The first time she had left the continental United States. Traveling had been on her bucket list, but she had never dreamed that her first interaction with the outside world would be in the ancient land of the Pharaohs. The trip came courtesy of a travel grant she won by casually surfing the internet and entering a contest late one night out of boredom. Maybe her luck was changing.

Celia felt as lucky as a rabbit with an amputated foot or a hoof-less horse getting a horseshoe nailed on. She needed a win because over the last few years she suffered some soul-shattering blows. First, she buried her father. He was one of the first victims of the pandemic. The pain of his sudden death almost took Celia to the grave with him.

Then, after an embarrassing meltdown at the office which ended with her screaming obscenities at her boss and security grabbing her by the elbow, she walked away from a decade long lucrative career and settled into a mediocre remote job where she could work pant-less in a t-shirt any time she wanted. Maybe the job change wasn't a loss but a much-needed transition. Sometimes peace of mind and being able to work in your underwear was worth a pay cut.

Next, her youngest child had entered college relinquishing himself from her maternal smothering, leaving her all alone after her husband of twenty-two years was no more. No, he was not dead, but she wished that he was. His death would have hurt much less than the knowledge that he lived across town in a high-tech high-rise where AI acted as his personal guard dog. There was no new woman. No change in sexual orientation. No new job. No new money. No midlife crisis. No sudden illness. Just a new life. A life without Celia.

Jason said he was simply tired of being married. He stated that he no longer wanted the responsibility of a wife; that he wanted to be married to himself. He told her to not take it personally because she was a wonderful woman and a good wife, and he was grateful for the years they shared together as if telling her that she was wonderful and good would lessen the blow of his rejection. He said he would like them to be friends. Despite Celia's protest and devastation, Jason filed for divorce and began living his new life without her. The sudden separation snatched her heart out of her chest, threw it into a blender, and poured the bloody goop down the sewer next to his offering of friendship.

Celia figured that Egypt was a gift from God letting her know that the universe still cared about her. But then again, when she first exited the airport, she stepped on a scarab beetle; its broken body smashed between the ground and her big toe which was poking too far out the front of her sandal. A hunched over old woman shrouded in black seemed to materialize near baggage claim beside Celia's suitcase which was missing a zipper. The old crone pointed to the beetle's gooey body and warned of bad luck.

"Come now!" the attractive tour guide said, breaking her from her thoughts.

A world-renowned archeologist and Egyptologist, Saqib Mohammad was golden skinned, middle-aged, and good-looking with a strong body. His Egyptian accent was sprinkled with a hint of a British brogue and his charm was as addictive as his kind eyes.

When Celia looked into his eyes, sometimes she imagined him naked, walking around her room; strong hairy legs and barrel chest heaving as his voice echoed with excitement telling her about the mysteries of Egypt. Other times, she felt a bit woozy, almost hypnotized. She had no idea why. She was not the kind of woman that lost her senses around attractive men. Afterall, she was an extremely attractive woman herself. Full-figured with thick wild hair and unblemished mahogany skin, there was no shortage of attractive men knocking on her door, except for Jason of course. But there was something different about Saqib. Something she could not put her finger on.

The entire group was sitting inside the motorboat, eyes glued to her face, waiting on her to come inside.

Celia coyly smiled at him, blinking profusely trying to stop sweat from pouring into her eyes. She was sure that there was nothing sexy about her eyeliner dripping down her cheeks like blobs of ink. Tomorrow, she planned to go makeup free.

The tour guide held out his arm to escort her onto the boat. She slipped her arm around his and stepped inside. The warmth of his skin shot electricity through her arm. She quickly let go and took a seat next to a handsome Nubian youth who was spreading out trinkets to sell to the passengers.

"Soon, we'll be arriving at the Philae Temple here in Aswan. The temple was dedicated to the goddess Iset or Aset better known as Isis," Saqib said as he pointed to the sand-colored structure peppered with palm trees surrounded by the fertile waters of the Nile.

Celia leaned back against the cushioned bench and watched the foamy waters of the Nile caress the side of the boat as it moved quickly towards the intricately carved temple.

The group disembarked from the boat; this time Celia was in the front of the line as they stepped onto the shore. Saqib stood waiting until the last passenger was on land. He beckoned everyone closer to him as he shared history about the monument and interesting pieces of the goddess myth. After educating, he told them to go and explore on their own and to meet at the small café on the edge of the temple in a half hour.

Celia sped off before Saqib could finish talking. She wanted to take as many pictures as possible while she examined each carving thoughtfully. As she walked, the warm wind rustled her maxi skirt blowing it like a rogue sail. She zigzagged through meandering tourists to get closer to the carved walls. Smiling, she ran her fingers across the face of the goddess Hathor. A familiarity filled Celia as she touched the carving.

"Beautiful, isn't it?" a voice whispered in her ear.

Celia jumped and spun around.

Saqib stood, a boyish grin on his face, his hands behind his back, his kind eyes smiling.

"You scared me," Celia confessed. "I didn't hear you walk up."

"You were so engulfed in the goddess, I'm sure you could hear nothing around you. Most people are more fascinated with Isis, yet here you are enthralled by the cow goddess. She is the protector of women and the goddess of pleasure," he replied, a mischievous look in his eyes. "Are you enjoying Egypt?"

"I am," Celia blushed.

"How long will you be visiting?" Saqib asked, his eyes locked on hers.

"I'll be flying back to Cairo in a couple of days then I'll be heading home this weekend," she answered.

"I live in Cairo. The tour will be ending soon. I'd love to give you a personal tour of Egypt," he smiled, his dark eyes almost magical with their everchanging shades of brown; his black hair floating upon the wind in whiffs of smoke -literal smoke. Celia blinked and focused until the ebony strands solidified once more. She chalked the phenomenon up as delirium due to heat.

"I'd like that," Celia said, her heart fluttering with elation and unease.

"Then it's a date," he exclaimed.

"I didn't say all that. Is it proper for Egyptians to date? Isn't dating a woman you have no intentions on marrying considered haram or shemal?" she laughed.

"Someone's been on the internet again," he scoffed trying to hide his annoyance behind a false smile.

"So, where are we going?" Celia asked.

"I'd like to take you to dinner then to see my personal collection of artifacts. Is that okay?" he asked as he reached out and touched her hair. The fluffy black spirals felt like cotton.

"You know you should ask before you touch a black woman's hair," Celia chided although the feeling of his fingers was pleasing, almost erotic.

Ignoring her comment, Saqib crossed his arms and waited for her to accept his invitation.

"Dinner sounds good. Hand me your phone," Celia said holding her hand out. Saqib dropped his cellphone into her palm and watched her as she typed and saved her contact information into his device. She handed the phone back to him and spun on her heels and walked off. It took every ounce of willpower for her not to look back over her shoulder. She could feel his eyes on her back as she walked away.

The flight from Aswan to Cairo was less than an hour. Celia grabbed her luggage from baggage claim only to discover a wheel was broken from the bottom of her suitcase and her handle was torn. She uttered a melodical sequence of profanity under her breath, cursed her luck, and marched out of the airport. Her rideshare was waiting for her to take her to her hotel.

Forty-five minutes later, Celia pulled up to a lush resort; its main building salmon colored and towering over the date palms surrounding it. A baggage porter removed her luggage from the vehicle and walked her to the customer service desk to check in. She was greeted by a smiling older gentleman, with twinkling eyes like her grandfather and toffee skin like her grandmother, who handed her keys and an entertainment schedule. Celia's luggage made it to her room before she did. She let herself in by tapping the key card to the door. Once inside, she fell across the bed like a dead woman and faded into the land of dream.

Tornadoes swirled around her. Desert sands met the horizon on every side. The stars flickered like millions of flashlights beaming on her skin; her skin shined like liquid copper. Paralyzed in a motionless purgatory, detached from the world around her yet embedded within it, statuesque she stood. Human and not. Trapped within the confines of her own body. Celia woke up; sweat streaming down her face. She ran her hands over her arms and legs ensuring that they were still flesh and blood. She let out a heavy sigh. It was only a dream.

For two days, she enjoyed endless meals, swam in one of the many pools in the resort, listened to live music and had strange dreams about paralysis every night. Celia wondered if her dreams were symbolic of the lack of fulfilment and progression in her life.

She marked the time by the Islamic calls to prayer that echoed through the city five times a day. She wrote about Egypt and all its wonders in her journal and sat on her balcony until the sweltering day faded into a cool breezy night.

The phone rang. Celia pushed open the balcony doors and walked into the room. She sat on the bed and looked at her cellphone. It was an international number. She swiped the screen and put the phone on speaker.

"Hello," she answered, allowing her tangerine sundress strap to fall off her shoulder as she leaned back against the headboard.

"Good evening, dear," Saqib greeted.

"Good evening," she replied.

"Are you ready to go?" he asked. "I'll be at your door in 5…4…3…2…"

A knock. She leapt up from the bed and opened the door.

Saqib stood in the hallway wearing a t-shirt that read "Amon-Min". Celia assumed it was the Arabic spelling for amen. She didn't really care what it meant so she didn't ask. The last thing she wanted to hear was the Egyptologist giving her a dissertation on how the sacred meaning of words can be lost in translation.

Saqib flashed a smile and waited until she invited him inside.

"Nice room," he complimented.

"Thanks. I'd invite you in, but I don't want you to get in trouble. Isn't it illegal for a man to be in a hotel room with a woman who is not his wife?" she asked.

Saqib rolled his eyes then stepped across the threshold.

Celia raised and dropped her shoulders. According to the internet, he was the one going to jail not her.

"I heard that this resort was nice," he said. "This is my first time visiting. I'll be sure to put this place on my list when I'm creating itineraries."

Celia slipped her feet in a pair of gold sandals, picked up a matching purse from the nightstand, and threw a shawl over her bare shoulders.

"I'm ready," she said.

A black sedan waited at the curb for the couple. A bellhop opened the car door and Saqib stepped aside for Celia to enter the vehicle then followed behind her. The car pulled off; wheels spinning like a racecar and headed for the expressway. Celia gasped. Saqib patted her arm and she felt instant calm.

Celia was in awe of the traffic. Cars seemed to drive in imaginary lanes which changed by the second. Every few miles there was a surprise: camels being transported, a donkey on the side of the road, a group of men hanging off the sides of a truck like they were seconds from falling to their deaths, a fearless woman, holding a baby a in one arm and a shopping bag in the other, sitting on the back of a speeding motorcycle, pedestrians crossing between moving vehicles. Celia thought the traffic in New York City was convoluted. Seeing the traffic in Cairo gave her a newfound respect for expert drivers.

Incomplete buildings towered over each side of the highway. Some of the buildings were nicely painted with ornate design elements. Others looked like they had survived a war. Saqib told her that they were family homes. They were built level by level and in accordance with the family's financial means.

The car pulled in front of what looked like an abandoned building save for a light on the far end. The couple exited the car, and a slew of street peddlers circled them like hyenas. Plastic deities, poorly sewn purses, wooden ankhs, and bottles of water were among the many items the peddlers tried to force into their hands. Saqib pushed through the merchants and asked Celia to ignore them as they entered the door of a brightly lit restaurant.

Immediately after they were seated, plates of hummus in a variety of flavors were set before them accompanied by flatbread, yellow rice, and a hot veggie tegan. Trays of lamb, chicken, and beef sausages were laid out before them. Celia ate until her stomach threatened to pop. Saqib watched her with sincerest amusement.

"Did you enjoy your dinner?" he asked while taking a napkin and wiping the side of her chin.

"I did," Celia smirked. "It was delicious. Where to now?"

"My place," he replied looking deeply into her eyes.

Hot flashes shot through her chest. She hadn't been with a man since her husband left more than a year ago, and the prospect of being with Saqib thrilled her but also made her nervous. She didn't know him or what kind of danger he could pose. With her luck, he would take her to the Nile, snatch her purse, and push her into the river.

"Calm down," he laughed. "I'm a good boy." Flames danced in his eyes.

Celia gulped. She wanted to believe him. Her body needed to believe him. It had been a long time since she had been plucked and pruned but there was something unsettling in his eyes, something ethereal almost.

"You're safe with me. I want to show you my collection of obscure artifacts. There's none like them in the entire world," he said, his smile cutting through all her inhibitions.

Celia forced herself to exhale. Her imagination was getting the best of her. Although thoughts of her being alone with

Saqib gave her pause, her curiosity and attraction to him prayed for the opportunity.

The couple exited the restaurant and entered the sedan again. The car pulled off, parting the street vendors like tangled hair. In no time, they pulled up in front of a beautiful apartment building with lush greenery framing its mihrab architecture.

"Come," Saqib invited extending his hand and helping her out of the car. They entered the building and ascended to the top floor. Saqib opened the apartment door. Modern leather furniture decorated the spacious living room. It was evident by the lack of color and the abundance of industrial art that a man lived there.

"Your apartment is lovely," she complimented.

"Thank you," he replied escorting her to the sofa and offering her a glass of wine.

She accepted.

Conversation flowed easily between them. They shared stories about their childhoods, families, education, careers, and dreams. They shared stories of humor and stories that greatly impacted their lives. The more they talked, the more the wine flowed. Serious conversation converted to uncontrollable giggling which led to excessive touching which led to heavy flirting which led to Saqib's mouth upon hers.

His lips were soft and hot. She drank from them greedily as they pressed upon her mouth and trailed down her neck. Sighs escaped her lips as his fingers ran down her torso. Her arms wrapped around his neck and her body pressed against his. Kisses were drizzled over her shoulders as Saqib knocked her shawl to the floor and unzipped her sundress. His thick hands caressed her back as his mouth found her breast. She cooed as his teeth brushed her nipples. Her dress hit the floor.

"Come with me," he commanded pulling her up from the sofa by the arm and towards a dark room at the end of the long hallway.

She followed obediently propelled by the concentrated desire burning through her thighs.

Celia felt that her luck was changing. She felt so fortunate to be in the home of such a magnetic man in one of the most exotic places in the world. If the sex was good, maybe next she'd win the lottery. Just in case her luck was still in shambles, she whispered a prayer for him to be sexually transmitted infection free and for him not to be dragging her into a sex dungeon filled with whips, chains, and pointy tipped tools.

Saqib turned on the light, illuminating the massive room. Crowns with bull horns hung on the walls. Golden baskets of prickly lettuce sat by the door. Spotlights shined over silver, gold, and bronze statues of women lining the walls. Women of all shapes and sizes. Beautiful women wearing the features of the world. Miniature statues of a man holding his ginormous phallus in his right hand and a flail held overhead in his left hand were scattered all over the room.

"Who is this?" Celia asked picking up one of the male figurines. She thumped its stone penis, which stuck out like a tree limb, and giggled.

"It's me, Min, of course," Saqib smirked and pointed to his t-shirt.

Celia raised her brow. If Saqib was packing like that statue, indeed, her luck had changed.

An empty alabaster platform stood on the far side of the room. A circular bed covered in red satin sat in the center of the room.

"What is this place?" Celia asked, taken aback by the lifelike artistry of the sculptures.

"My very own temple of goddesses," he replied pulling her further into the room.

"There are none like them in all the world. Some are more than five thousand years old; others are brand new."

Celia approached the nearest statue, the marble floor cold under her feet. The details of the statue were remarkable. Tiny hairs, pores, wrinkles, and nails were all perfectly rendered. Even the eyes seemed to follow her as she moved about the room.

"Where did you find them?" she asked touching the arm of one of the golden sculptures. It was warm. Celia figured the high beaming spotlights warmed the metal. "They look so real."

"They seem to find me," he said.

Saqib gave her a moment to further explore, then, pulled her down onto the bed, sliding her lace underwear off with one calculated pull. He undressed himself with a sense of urgency as if she would run away before his shirt hit the floor. His body was thick and strong, just like she imagined it.

His mouth was upon hers again, this time wet, aggressive, and all tongue. Celia tried to catch her breath but each time she inhaled the wind was sucked out of her. Saqib suckled her breasts then migrated south until his kisses rained between her legs. Before she could fully embrace the pleasure of his tongue, he mounted her, thrusting himself into her like a fist through a wall before she could request a condom. She moaned with trepidation and excitement as he rocked her body to climax. Little death seized her. She fell limp in his arms, unable to lift her head, her arms, her legs. She was spent. Her body pulsated from head to toe.

"Bear my sons, my queen!" Saqib commanded as he continued to thrust. His body sliding into her, coaxing her from her respite into an effortless rhythm matching his own. Her legs wrapped around his torso as her tongue traced his collar bone and her fingers dug into his back. Orgasm upon orgasm pulsated through her hips in waves of unbridled electricity. With each contraction, she wanted to pledge her life to him. With each thrust, her lust morphed into love, the most toxic carnal adoration her heart could muster.

"I can't," she whined. "I wish I could," she cooed. Ecstasy grabbed her so hard that she thought her insides might bruise. In that moment, she would bare him a thousand children if she could, but she could not. She had tubal ligation surgery after her son was born. Jason wanted no more children. She didn't either until now.

Mid-stroke, Saqib froze, arching backwards -the back of his head brushing the top of his buttocks like a boneless serpent knotting itself. His skin shifted from tan to burgundy to pitch black.

Celia squealed in terror, her arms and legs flailing, her hands beating upon his chest. She writhed and clawed but could not break free from his embrace. He squeezed her, his powerful arms rendering her helpless. Celia felt her spine would crack. She whimpered.

Saqib let out a deep primal moan -the sound of Uranus being castrated by Cronus. A wave of liquid heat shot through Celia's womb. Her body dropped to the bed like a dead thing. Smoldering lava coursed through her veins. Burning sensations spread from her womb in orgasmic waves to her thighs, up her stomach, through her arms and legs, then up her neck. Her joints stiffened like her cartilage had transformed into concrete.

Saqib stood up and backed away from the bed, his eyes -full flames now, his hair -tongues of smoke dancing from his scalp.

"What's happening to me? What are you?" Celia cried, her mahogany skin taking on a metallic sheen; the burning sensation deepening into a hot ache simultaneously pulsing through her body.

"What did you do to me?" she cried, her body feeling cold and unattached. Too heavy to move, she searched Saqib's expressionless face for answers.

"I'm sorry my love," Saqib whispered as he straightened her arms and legs like one would do a life-sized doll. "I wanted you to bear mighty gods, but your body could not. Your body absorbed the treasures of my essence. Now you will be my treasure forever. One of my goddesses for all time."

He turned her face towards him, smoothing away her panicked expression and wiping away her tears. He combed her hair with his fingers, creating a tamed intentional wildness.

Out of the corner of Celia's eye she noticed one of the statues of the well-endowed deities. She looked to Saqib then back to the statue. Saqib's skin, like the statue, dark as soot; penis erect; hair standing up like the crown of Horas. They were one in the same, Amon-Min, the god of fertility.

Celia screamed out. There was no sound. Her body was no longer her own but a metal shell housing her spirit. Tears fell from her eyes and became solidified metal upon her cheeks.

Saqib lifted her body from the bed and placed her on an empty platform on the far side of the room.

"Beautiful," he whispered as he looked upon Celia's bronze body standing on the platform, a new goddess in his temple. He gathered their clothes, walked out of the door, and turned off the light.

Celia screamed silently, suddenly aware that she was not screaming alone. Like the women incased in their own bodies around her, her luck had completely run out.

Panola Mountain

"Summers in Atlanta are hot and muggy. I imagine the heat feels like a wool straitjacket, better yet, a cheap polyester catsuit," Joshua quipped as he walked up the dirt path with his date Imani whom he had met a few nights ago in a bar in East Atlanta Village.

He had noticed her across the room dancing with a group of girls like she had never been anywhere in her life. Arms flailing, hips pumping, neck rolling, her awkward dance moves reminded him of an exotic mating ritual he saw two birds perform on the Animal Channel. Her unbashful self-confidence made him smile. It was refreshing to see a woman so comfortable in her skin. He loved her medium brown skin tone and wild natural hair that was cropped on the sides and spiraled high on the top of her head like a bouquet of sandy brown curly fries. Minimal makeup, and a free-flowing sundress that highlighted just enough of her body to let him know that her figure was full in all the right places seduced him from his corner of the room into hers.

Joshua approached her with a friendly hello followed by a generous round of drinks and eats for her and her friends. The connection was instant. Conversation flowed as if they had been friends for years, so he asked her out on a date. He decided on a hiking adventure because he remembered her telling her friends how much she loved the summer sun. Growing up in the coastal area of Alaska denied her all the hot summer fun she had witnessed on TV. Immediately after asking her on a date, Joshua decided to take her to Panola Mountain State Park in Stockbridge, a suburban area in metro Atlanta. A week later, here they were panting and sweating up the heavily forested path.

Joshua regretted taking her hiking the moment that he realized his underarm sweat had made giant circles on the armpits of his T-shirt. He pushed the straps of his backpack deep into his pits to camouflage the widening wetness. Being an Atlanta native, he should have known better than sweating and panting up the side of a mountain in the middle of July; especially while entertaining an interesting woman. He prayed that the smell of his sweat was an aphrodisiac instead of a repellent.

Imani laughed. She wiped the pooling perspiration from her forehead with the back of her hand and smiled. She felt like Supergirl, drawing energy from the sun, and becoming more invigorated by the minute. Her red, yellow, and blue spandex outfit helped with her superhero vibe.

"I'd rather have a hot and muggy summer than one drenched in ice," Imani replied as she stepped over a twisting tree branch laying across the grassy path. "I don't ever want to live in the cold again. Black people are tropical people!" she laughed. "I don't know what possessed my father to house me and my mother in the arctic."

"Probably the money," Joshua replied blinking rapidly trying to propel salty sweat from his dark brown eyes.

"True," Imani agreed. "My father was able to stack a lot of money while living in that ice cold hell."

"I take it that an Alaskan cruise is out of the question," Joshua joked. "Well, you won't have to worry about freezing to death in Atlanta. It gets cold, but it never stays cold for long. You can pretty much wear the same clothes all year around. Just add a coat. We have all four seasons. I appreciate that about this place."

"Were you born here?" she asked while plucking a yellow flower and placing it behind her ear. The smell of it permeated her nostrils and faded.

"Beautiful," he sighed as he looked at the floral accent in her hair.

She smiled. He smiled too, revealing deep dimples in each cheek.

"Yes, I was born here and grew up here. Can't you tell by the t-shirt?" he pointed to his t-shirt which read *ATL HOE*.

Imani shook her head and laughed at the two words printed in giant bold letters. She wasn't offended by the popular phrase used by locals to punctuate their city patriotism.

"But I moved to California after college and stayed there for about five years; then, I moved to Mississippi for two years, and Florida for a year and a half. After working and saving, I was able to leave my job and start a successful data consulting firm. I moved back home to Atlanta about three years ago. There's no place like home," he said as he stopped and clicked his heels three times.

Imani immediately picked up on the reference and laughed aloud.

"Were you born in Alaska?" Joshua asked.

Imani replied, "Yep. Born and raised. I escaped to New York during college and lived there for a decade until recently. I let my cousin talk me into moving to *The Black Mecca*." Imani used air quotes when saying *The Black Mecca*. She continued, "I'm single with no children, and in between jobs, so I figured it was worth a shot."

"What do you do?" he asked as he picked up a large stick and began to use it as a staff.

"You look like Gandalf the Gray," she laughed.

He held up the stick and yelled, "You shall not pass!"

Their echoing laughs were answered with the sound of whispering insects, singing birds, and conspiring squirrels. Animal noises filled the space around them as they walked slowly up the incline.

Panola Mountain was a strange kind of mountain. It did not visually stand high like most imposing mountainous structures. It couldn't be seen from the street nor from inside the park. One only became aware of its height when reaching the top and looking down upon the vast landscape beneath or spying the full glory of the Atlanta skyline shining in the distance.

"Are you sure that this is a mountain instead of a big hill?" Imani asked as she picked up an acorn and threw it at a huge neon green grasshopper clinging to a tree a couple of yards in front of them. The grasshopper jumped away and vanished into a nearby bush.

"Leave that bug alone," Joshua laughed. "It ain't bothering you!"

"It was bothering me!" she replied chuckling. "The thought of that giant thing landing in my hair is horrific!"

Joshua shook his head and laughed at her once again. He understood her concern because he was secretly afraid of huge hopping bugs too. There was something about things that jumped that made him want to run home screaming, but he couldn't share that. He was a man, and he was sure that no woman wanted a man who would run from bugs faster than she would. Men were predestined to be brave against six legged monsters whether they feared them or not.

"Let's go this way," Joshua suggested when they came to a fork in the path. The park sign told him to go in the opposite direction, but he felt a bit rebellious. It seemed as if the foliage was greener, and the sunlight sparkled against the leaves sprinkling everything in splendor in the direction that he chose.

"Are you sure?" Imani asked. "You're not going to lead me off the edge of this invisible mountain, are you?"

"Never," he replied and winked. Joshua held out his midnight black hand, interlocking his fingers with hers, and she hesitantly followed him down the unknown path.

"Useless fact," Imani stated randomly. "Did you know that panola is the Choctaw word for cotton?"

"I did not know that," Joshua confessed with a grin on his clean-shaven face. "Why do you know that?"

"I enjoy trivia and I read an absorbent amount," said Imani. "My head is filled with all sorts of useless information."

"You seem to have a lot of leisure time," Joshua replied with one eyebrow raised. "What did you say you did again?"

"I didn't say," Imani retorted and raised her eyebrow in reply. "At the moment, I am enjoying my life until I find something that brings me joy. I taught elementary school for a while then became burned out. Then I tried on a few professions trying to find a good fit. I've worked as a life coach, an herbalist, a dance teacher, owned a bakery, and also a self-proclaimed anthropologist and folklorist. Now, I'm here in Atlanta trying to find something new to do."

"Very interesting," Joshua replied sincerely. He admired her free spirit and willingness to explore new things. He wished that he had the luxury to change jobs on a whim.

He hoped that she could truly afford to live her life on a whim and that he was not courting an unemployed sofa surfer. It was not that he cared about how much money she made. He made enough for the both of them and a couple people more, but it was important that he dated a woman with her own purpose and passion.

"Living in Alaska made my father very wealthy and being his only child, in turn made me very wealthy as well. Wealth gives me the freedom to explore different options," Imani said.

"That's pretty cool, but what are you passionate about?" he asked, his tone a bit more serious than it had been all day.

"I'm passionate about life," she answered. "I'm passionate about exploring the world and discovering the miracles hidden in the depths of it. Work is not passion. Work is a way to earn. I am rich and I'm smart. My money makes money while I sleep. I don't want to work. I want to learn. I want to help people. I want to witness the holy and the profane so I can be sure of the difference. I want to truly experience life with all five of my senses. That's what I am passionate about."

Joshua nodded and smiled. Imani was unlike anyone he had ever encountered. Her zest for life made him want to journey with her.

The couple walked for about ten minutes until they came to a large clearing under a tightly intertwined canopy of trees. A circle of misshapen rocks surrounded a patch of glowing purple flowers. What appeared to be a trillion lightening bugs hovered over the gleaming blossoms -the smell of them was like honey cakes.

Imani gasped. She said, "I've never seen fireflies glow like this in the daytime. This is amazing!"

Joshua nodded in agreement as he stared at the glittering swarm.

"Do you hear that?" he inquired.

"Hear what?" Imani replied.

"Shhhh. Listen closely," he said sweetly.

Imani leaned her head to the side and listened intensely.

Instead of buzzing, there was music. A strange music that brought to mind the sound of stringed instruments and wooden flutes. Strange music that defied human ability to play in such a whimsical and low pitch descant. Music that floated from the glowing patch on melodic wings into their ears.

"Wow," Imani whispered. "I've never heard anything like this."

"Me either," Joshua replied as he stepped closer to the levitating luminous orchestra.

As he approached, the swarm divided into two clouds of light and out of the middle of the flower patch stepped two identical, save for their skin tones, female creatures. One was Carolina blue and the other sapphire blue. Golden eyes stared out from valentine shaped faces. Clouds of big black hair bounced off their shoulders as if a tiny wind blew just for them. Leaves and flowers were their garments draping them in robes of fragrant color. Fluttering amethyst metallic wings protruded from their backs. Standing about four feet tall, the creatures said in unison, "Welcome to our mountain."

Imani blinked her eyes. She asked, "What did you put in those brownies you gave me in the car?"

"Milk chocolate and walnuts," Joshua answered blinking slowly.

"Do you see what I see?" Imani asked; her eyes glued to the blue fairies standing right in front of them.

Joshua nodded.

"I think we should leave," Imani urged as she squeezed his hand as tight as she could.

Joshua said nothing. His unblinking eyes locked with the fairies. He shook his hand loose from Imani's.

"Come with us," the fairies implored; their fingers beckoning the couple to come forward. "Joshua, we have been waiting for you."

Joshua walked slowly towards the flower patch, still unblinking.

"Joshua, I think we should go," Imani spat through her teeth, not taking her eyes off the fairies who were now circling Joshua like technicolored vultures and pulling him towards the flower patch.

"Joshua!" Imani screamed as Joshua's feet touched the flower patch and he and the fairies vanished.

■■

"Where am I?" Joshua asked as he looked around.

Mushrooms the size of cars and flowers the size of buses were everywhere. The strong floral aroma almost made him gag. Blades of grass as thick as tree trunks surrounded him like a jail cell.

"Where am I?" Joshua screamed aloud. There was no answer. There was no sound. No sound at all. Silence. Dead silence.

Days went by, maybe weeks, maybe months, maybe years in the silence. There was no way he could possibly know. The sun never set in the mysterious realm he found himself trapped in. Joshua sat behind the grass bars thinking of ways to escape to no avail. His mind threatened to spiral into chaos. He filled his stomach with berries that grew next to a clear pond inside the grassy cage. He passed time counting leaves and making rock formations out of pebbles.

"Let me go!" Joshua yelled as loud as his voice could elevate. "I want to go home!"

The fairies appeared, startling him so badly that he fell backwards.

"Where am I?" he asked as he got back on his feet.

"Panola Mountain," they replied.

"I want to leave," he said, his brows furrowing, his fists balled, and his teeth clenched.

"Not yet," they replied. "We have a gift for you."

The fairies revealed hands full of silver mushrooms.

"Eat," they demanded. "Eat and see what we see."

"What is it?" he asked leery of their intentions.

"It will open your eyes," they replied.

"My eyes are already open," he said.

"No, they aren't. We want you to truly see. You are a good man. Your great great grandfather Tom left this gift for you. He knew you would come one day. Take it!" they urged.

"I never knew my great great grandfather Tom. He disappeared years before my great grandfather was born. Family legend said that because Tom was a powerful preacher who educated and liberated a lot of black people, he was probably caught and hanged by the Klan," said Joshua.

"No such thing happened," the fairies laughed. "He climbed this mountain, and he chose to stay here with us. He was weary of fighting an uphill battle. Tom told us that it was easier to light a fire with two wet sticks than to change the hearts of evil people," they said hovering over Joshua like mystical birds. "You can choose to stay here too."

"No thank you," Joshua replied. "Let me out of this cage."

"It's only grass. You can leave at any time. Your imprisonment is in your mind," they said.

Joshua walked over to one of the blades and touched it. It bent easily under the weight of his hand. He whispered a profanity. He felt like an idiot for not even trying before.

"Where is Tom now?" Joshua inquired as he walked through the grass circle that he thought was his cage onto a pebbled path.

"With your ancestors," they said.

"You mean dead!" Joshua snapped.

Anxiety swelled in his chest. There was a chance that the fairies meant to force him to join his ancestors as well.

"Death does not exist," they replied. "We only want you to see."

"See what?" he asked as he walked. He stopped at a pond and watched winged toads hop and fly across crystal-like lily pads.

"See things as they actually are. See that life is a miracle. Life is a gift and every moment of it should be savored," they answered as they whirred around him.

"If I eat, will you take me back?" Joshua asked, his voice cracking and a bit high pitched. He hated to admit it to himself, but he was scared. He didn't want to die in Never Never Land or whatever this Godforsaken place was.

"Yes," they replied. "We will take you back."

"Promise?" he asked, his voice quaking as he extended his hand. The fairies dropped the metallic mushrooms into his palm.

"We promise," they replied, eyes turning like spinning wheels of flame.

Joshua took a deep breath and ingested the mushrooms. His eyes shot open.

"Joshua!" Imani screamed. "Where are you?"

"I'm right here," Joshua replied as he sat up in the middle of the no longer luminescent flower patch, violet petals stark against his dark skin. The flickering musical lights were gone. The honey cake smell was gone. The fairies were gone.

Imani ran over to him and caressed his face with her hand. His smooth-shaven face was now adorned with a silver and ebony beard, thick and curly. His tight young skin showed a tinge of age by way of crow's feet and tiny creases around his mouth.

"How long was I gone?" Joshua asked, confused by Imani wearing the same outfit she had on when he had left ages ago. He was even more confused by the bright blue aura that surrounded her body.

"Only a few minutes," she replied as she helped him get to his feet. "What happened to you?"

"I don't know," he replied as his eyes adjusted to the world around him. Everything was alive. Even the trees seemed to breathe. Insects swarmed around in logical patterns that he had never noticed before. Sunbeams sparkled like liquid diamonds dripping on the earth. He looked up at the sky and saw that the pollution particles of chemtrails were simply jet fuel exhaust and not some sort of mind control spray. He wondered how many other conspiracy theories his new vision would help him debunk or prove. *What if the King of England really was a lizard?* He laughed to himself and shook off the absurd thought.

"Are you okay?" Imani asked, dusting clinging petals from his shorts and the back of his t-shirt.

"I don't know. I don't know," he repeated, "but I'm excited to find out. I want you to see what I see."

"What do you see?" she asked, while watching him stare off into the sky like it was a brand-new thing to behold.

Joshua opened one of his hands and revealed a few silver mushrooms.

"Here," he said. "Eat it."

Imani took the mushrooms and rolled them around in her palm for a while. She looked up into his eyes and decided to trust him. After all, life was about taking chances.

Imani placed the metallic fungi upon her tongue and swallowed. She swooned. Unknown colors streamed into her eyes. She gasped at the beauty of the world around her. A bright yellow aura enveloped Joshua. Her eyes were opened.

"Let's go live that life you were telling me about," he said as he grabbed her hand and they quickly descended Panola Mountain.

Tony V

Tony IV expired last year. When his chip short circuited, I felt like my soul fizzled with it in a loud pop and a bright flash of light which culminated in months of darkness. Sad, crippling darkness. Lonely, suffocating darkness.

Tony IV was the perfect android. His skin was soft and lifelike; his facial expressions thoughtful and sincere; the gait of his walk and the smoothness of his movements were as human as an organic human. When he kissed my lips and held my hand, I knew in my heart that a real soul did not dwell within his hard drive, but I had no idea how another robot could be built so remarkably close to my organic husband.

Tony models I-III were fetish toys at best, each model more advanced than the last. They were good for daily tasks and mild pleasures, nothing more. But when Tony IV arrived, my heart leapt within my chest. I thought I had seen a ghost when he knocked on my door. His sienna skin and dimpled cheeks gave me chills. A crooked smile revealed flawless white teeth and his wild kinky hair made me gasp. My husband was standing before me; all six feet, one hundred and eighty pounds of him. Tony

IV was an exact replica, right down to his voice, of the love of my life -Tony. Tony IV was Tony's true doppelganger, but no matter how advanced, a machine could never be a man. It could never be the man who I raised children with, the man who I fought back-to-back with during the first alien invasion, the man who housed one of my kidneys, and the man who stayed by my side through every sickness and death of our loved ones.

It could never be Tony. It could never be the man who had died of the Purple Plague over a decade ago; a victim of germ warfare; one of billions who had perished.

The germ wars started in 2020 with a virus that ripped through the world and killed a little less than five percent of the population. The world went into a panic not knowing the true tragedy that lurked in the future. Fifty years later, another disease was unleashed upon the people by greedy world leaders vying for power. They didn't learn from the pandemic that disease could not be contained, nor did they learn to respect the sanctity of life during the worldwide massacres of the alien invasions. Human unity was short lived. In trying to eliminate their enemies, greedy opportunists nearly eliminated us all with the Purple Plague.

The Purple Plague ate into the flesh of the human population with its pulsating boils and thirty-five percent survival rate until the human population dwindled into a quarter of what it had previously been. Devastation, starvation, and disease wiped out most of North and South America and Europe. Africa and Asia retained most of their population because of the strict travel guidelines and air-based forcefields that locked their borders away from noncitizens. Also, the banning of chemicals in food helped their citizens build stronger immune systems while the rest of the world fed on lab produced foods saturated by cancer causing chemicals.

By 2100, Kwanwee, a large country covering the entire coast of West Africa, became the strongest world power. Its technology, spiritual power, natural medical advancements, and military were beyond comparison. They gained their power by abandoning synthetic medicines and returning to the healing properties of the earth. Their laboratories became immense gardens, and their industrialized cities became simple villages that no longer contaminated the earth. Better food and health tripled the lifespan of humanity. Growing old gracefully was an understatement.

The Oniwosan, powerful physicians, used spiritual energy and science to wipe the deadliest diseases from the planet. Their spirit power fueled their military. Where other countries fought with bullets and bombs, Kwanwee's army enlisted their ancestors, the Olo, who could not die nor be harmed.

Summoned through sacred ritual and dance, the Olo fought with lightning bolts and darkness. If death did not come through their electric touch, it came through the melodic spells which thundered from their lips casting their enemies into black holes of nothingness. The music of death, outsiders called it. It was the drumbeat of the damned.

Although benevolent, the Kwanwee ruled the world with an iron fist. Even my small corner of the world where the seal of Kwanee is on every microchip used to buy and sell. We speak their language and don their clothes. We adhere to their philosophies and honor their ancestors because they are the ancestors of us all.

I live in what is left of what used to be the United States of America. Now it is a wilderness of small tribes littering the land from coast to coast; a total population of about 50,000 humans and 400,000 androids. I live in the southeast region of the country in an enormous city of a thousand humans and 28,000 androids.

Although Asia is the largest manufacturer of androids, Africa, especially Kewanee, is the primary manufacturer of luxury androids. Androids are so lifelike that the only way to tell them apart from humans is the tiny skin tone button located behind their right ear. Honestly, I have not seen another human in so long, I can barely tell the difference between a mole and a button. Long ago, I saved enough money to send my children and their families to Kewanee to live among flesh and blood.

I sit in my pod and look in the mirror as I anticipate the delivery of the next addition of my husband. I hope that the new bot will be as organic looking as Tony IV.

Age decorates my face with laugh lines and a faint hint of crows' feet. I think I look pretty good for a hundred- and fifteen-year-old woman considering I have birthed six children, fought in two wars, built my home with my own two hands, and survived a broken heart. My copper skin is taut and smooth for the most part. My dreadlocks are thick, waist length, and chestnut colored like my eyes. Yeah, I look pretty darn good. I hope my new husband will share the same sentiment. If he doesn't, I'll just program him too.

I push a button on my pod and my face is airbrushed with red for my lips and black liner for my eyes. I smile and get up and start to pace the floor. Tony V was supposed to be delivered hours ago! I check my transport unit, but there are no incoming alerts, so I decide to search the information system. With a wave of my hand, a hologram of a large screen appears in the middle of the room. I take a deep breath and center my being. Searching the WIE (World Information Edifice) with a cluttered mind could mean disaster because the system connects the minds of humans with the hard drive of the world computer. Think the wrong thought and the end may come.

I focus and allow my thoughts to merge with the information system. My soul source intermarries with the computer and my inner desires are displayed upon the screen. I search the system for tracking information. It says that my package is on the way, so I calm down and allow my imagination to wonder. As I wonder, I pray. I pray for my new android to be more than a help but a companion. I miss the organic energy of human flesh. I envy the Africans and Asians because they are still residing in organic communities, yet they lock us out of their lands, unless we can pay handsomely. They feel we should be grateful because they supply us with toys.

As I search the WIE, I stumble upon a poem. A strange little poem that I assume is meant to be used as a blessing over an android. I have never seen a blessing for a machine. The poem is strange indeed. It was written by an Oniwosan, a sympathizer perhaps. The name below the poem is similar to my son's. My heart flutters. It couldn't be! Could it? The words of the Oniwosan are forbidden to those who are not Oniwosan so seeing the poem is alarming. Oniwosan words are much too powerful to be shared on the WIE, too powerful to be uttered. Oniwosan words uttered become life; tangible life. I want to turn away and report the poem to the authorities, but the lyrics draw me in. I can hear the lyrics being sung in my head although they are only words on a holographic screen. A choir of voices sing in my brain, a chant that channels my progenitors, an ode to creation, a song of integration, of spirit and machine in coitus, of metal and flesh, death and life. It sings in voices known and unknown to me. I sing along, loud, and strong. The words are implanted in my heart. The air around me is alive with electricity. Tingling sensations jets in and out my pores. I close my eyes. When I open them, the words are gone.

A bright light flickers in the corner of the room. A robotic voice echoes, "Incoming! Incoming!" as a tunnel made of light takes shape. I rush over to my transporter and wait until the light stops flickering. When it does, my husband's robotic twin is standing in front of me like a man frozen in time. I embrace his cheek then press the button behind his right ear. Tony V opens his eyes and smiles. He holds out his hand, palm up, waiting for me to program him. His palm changes from flesh into a small keyboard and screen with a settings menu on it. Before I push the first button, the song comes back into my heart.

I kiss Tony V's still lips and whisper the poem into his mouth. I chant my prayer and give a dead thing breath. I sing into its ears and allow the mental rhythm to move my limbs to its magical beat. A strange orange glow covers the android and disperses like tangerine worms burrowing into the walls. There's a glint in his empty eyes. He inhales then exhales.

I grab my chest. After all I have been through, my heart threatens to stop right when I am on the precipice of discovery. How could a machine draw breath?

Tony V steps away from me and looks down at his hands as if he had never seen such a thing. He looks up at me then around the room in a confused excitement.

I gasp. I know in my heart it's *him*. I can feel it like one feels the wind. I open my mouth, but nothing happens.

"Tony?" I force out. The words falling from my lips like half chewed food.

"Hey baby," he says as he walks over to me with a slight strut, head up and shoulders back.

I know that walk anywhere. It reminds me of ancient movie stars. It is a walk like Super Fly and Denzel Washington created an android baby. It was Tony's walk. The real Tony.

He wraps his arms around me.

A tear falls from my eye.

He brushes it away and say, "I've missed you."

Daphine

"You really have a type. You know that?" Zenobia asked as she tossed a fried shrimp into her highly glossed mouth and tossed the tail onto the edge of her dinner plate. She wiped her mouth; brown foundation and glittery lip gloss covered the napkin like sparkling mud thick with mica.

"My type is my business," Daphine retorted, leaning back in her chair, and allowing her eyes to take note of every older gentleman in the room.

"I'm not trying to get in your business but you're piping hot, well-to-do, and cool as hell. Why do you date geriatric white men? By looks, your last date was at least eighty! Atlanta is full of fine men of every color. I'm not saying that you have to date a brother, but old Jim Crow looking men are not the move. A matter of fact, even when we were young you were picking up men twenty to thirty years our senior. Why them? Didn't yo' mama tell you that old men will give you worms?" Zenobia asked before taking a long sip of a turquoise blue cocktail with a rainbow umbrella leaning off the rim.

"Again, my business," Daphine snapped. She crossed her long yellow legs and let her high heel swing on the tip of her toes.

"I told you that my husband Van's business partner Christavius is crazy about you," Zenobia said. "He's your age, handsome, spiritual, financially stable, straight, and kind. His ex-girlfriend used to work with me. She told everyone that he's the reason why she's bowlegged," Zenobia laughed aloud. "He's a catch girl. If I were single, I would date him or at least take his stick shift for a test drive!"

"How can he be crazy about me? He doesn't even know me," Daphine chuckled, still scoping the bar for men.

"He met you last year at the Christmas party at my house. Ya'll danced together all night long. He even made your evil behind smile," Zenobia jested.

Daphine laughed too. She remembered him. She liked him, but he was not who she was looking for.

"I think you should give the man a chance. There's no reason to be alone for the rest of your life. The last time you were really happy was when you were a kid," Zenobia said, the mirth sucked from her voice like a syringe. "That was over forty years ago Daphine. Let the past go. We ain't getting any younger. The time for fun is now."

Daphine's eyes went dark. Over forty years ago was the last time she had seen her twin brother, Davante', alive. A tightness in her chest made her gasp and exhale slowly trying to banish the emotional pain that throbbed within her.

"Bingo," Daphine whispered and sat up quickly pushing away all thoughts of her twin brother. She pulled her shoe onto her heel and stood up.

"That's him," a voice whispered.

"I'll pay for your food. You can leave when you're done. I'll not be leaving alone tonight," Daphine said confidently, adjusting her dress. "Talk to you later Zenobia. Love you lots!" Daphine kissed her friend on the cheek and left the table taking slow sensual steps towards a liver spotted old man sitting at the bar.

Zenobia let out a sigh and rolled her eyes before she crunched on another shrimp.

"Anyone sitting here?" Daphine asked, her voice soft and sensuous, leaning so close to the older man that her lips brushed his ear.

He looked up at her, shocked to see a vibrant light-skinned black woman with thick curly red hair and a seductive smile.

"N…n..no one is sitting here. P..p…please join me," he stuttered, pulling the barstool out for her to sit down.

"What's a sophisticated young man doing here alone?" Daphine asked as she looked into the old man's graying blue eyes. Cataracts bit at the edges of his irises. A hairy mole sat high on his cheek. Canyons of wrinkles were carved on every inch of his face.

The man smiled, the pink skin around his mouth curling.

"Would you like a drink?" he asked smiling with a mouth full of teeth all the exact same size and shape like yellowing ceramic rectangles glued together.

"No thank you," she sweetly declined. "Are you married?"

The old man hesitated. His eyes told her that he was.

"It doesn't matter," she said. "What's one night?" She smiled, running her tongue over her teeth.

The old man swallowed hard as she stood up from her stool and extended her hand to him. He accepted, stood up, and followed her out of the bar.

+ + +

"Earlier tonight, the body of seventy-five-year-old real estate mogul, Richard Kramer, was found in the front seat of his car with his throat slashed and a mysterious marking carved into his chest. Witnesses say that he was last seen leaving a popular upscale Atlanta bar with a younger woman. He leaves behind his wife of thirty years and four adult children. Investigators say that this is the seventh victim of what authorities call the A-town Massacres in the last four years bearing the same marking," Aashvi Patel, a veteran news reporter reported through the flat-screen television hanging above the fireplace in Daphine's master bedroom. "The FBI has been called to aid in the investigation. Atlanta hasn't seen serial killings of this magnitude since the Atlanta Child Murders circa 1979-1981."

"He got what he deserved," a voice whispered.

Daphine turned off the TV and climbed into bed.

A heavy knock made her front door vibrate.

Daphine threw her legs over the side of the bed and slid her feet into a pair of satin slippers then grabbed the matching robe which hung on the back of the door. Dragging her feet, she made her way to the front door.

"Who is it?" Daphine asked through the thick wooden door, knowing exactly who it was.

"Kat."

Daphine opened the door and stepped aside to let a tiny, frail, blue-haired woman into the apartment. Her skin was pale and clinging to her bones. Thick white whiskers dotted both corners of her lips. Bulky dentures filled her small mouth. Hunched back and slow-walking, Katherine O'Hara, better known as Ms. Kat, took nearly two minutes to cross the threshold. At a hundred and nine years old, she remained a beautiful woman full of creativity and tenacity. Head of the apartment welcome committee, a choir member at church, and the sharpest shooter on this side of the Mason Dixon, Kat was a hardcore feminist, a vicious advocate for human rights, and a widow whose adoring husband died two-decades earlier. She lived alone in the apartment across the hall but made a welcomed appearance in Daphine's living room at least thrice weekly.

"What are you doing out so late Ms. Kat?" Daphine asked the elderly woman who was now sitting on the edge of a nearby chair.

"It's only eight o'clock my dear. The moon is barely out," Kat said in a voice rich with age. "I just came to tell you that my son Bobby is coming to stay with me for a couple of weeks so if you see a man going in and out of my apartment next month, you know who it is. I don't want you to worry my dear. You look out for me so well."

Daphine smiled and squeezed the old woman's hand.

"I'm glad you told me. You know I don't play about your safety Ms. Kat. You're like my nanna," Daphine said sincerely. Her blood-related grandparents meant everything to her when they were alive. Their wisdom and understanding brought her profound stability for the first half of her life. Now all of them were deceased and Ms. Kat helped fill a void in Daphine's heart.

"I know dear," replied Kat. "I want you to meet him. I warn you; he can be unpleasant at times because he idolized my politically incorrect brutish father, but like dad, in his heart, he's a good boy. Will you come to lunch with us?"

"Of course, I will," Daphine agreed. "Set the date and time and I'll be there."

+   +   +

A short stocky doorman with olive skin and long blonde hair opened the door to Southern Elect, an elite country club for a diversity of Atlanta socialites and frequented by local celebrities and the bourgeoisie. Daphine, Zenobia, Van, and Christavius stepped inside.

Normally Daphine didn't have the stomach for such pretentious places, but her best friend begged her to go so there she was dressed to kill and apparently on a double date.

"I'm glad you agreed to come with us," Zenobia whispered into Daphine's ear as they walked into a grand ballroom decorated in lush fabrics, fragrant blossoms, ornate furniture, and angular chandeliers.

"How can I say no? You pestered me for weeks," Daphine replied. "Did I really have a choice after you threatened to come to my house and drag me out by my hair?"

Zenobia laughed, "You know I would have done it too!"

The couples found their table. Christavius pulled out Daphine's chair then sat down beside her.

"Thank you," she said avoiding his eyes.

Kind, amber, and long lashed, his penetrating eyes made her stomach flip. Daphine had to keep her focus. He was not who she was looking for tonight.

"You're welcome," he replied.

A server came to the table almost immediately offering champagne, fresh fruit, and hors d' oeuvres.

Zenobia filled her plate with tasty bites.

Daphine declined everything but the champagne.

"It's been a long time since I've seen you," Christavius said, smiling big and wide. His handsome face was pleasant and his cologne intoxicating.

"Yes, it has been quite a while," Daphine agreed unable to squelch the smile taking over her face. She had to admit to herself that Christavius was charming.

"Did ya'll hear about that man that got murdered last month?" Van asked while swallowing a whole strawberry.

Daphine was mentally preparing to do the Heimlich maneuver in case Van fell over the side of the table.

Christavius' smile vanished. He turned his attention from Daphine to Van.

"Yes," Christavius replied. "My firm is handling that case. The victim's family is suing the nightclub he was parked outside of for having inadequate security."

"The man that got killed kinda looked like the old coot that Daphine left the club with when we went out last month," Zenobia laughed. She bit into a strawberry then fed one to her husband.

Daphine rolled her eyes and took a sip of champagne.

"There's nothing funny about what happened to that man," Christavius scolded. "He was butchered. No one deserves to die like that. No one."

Zenobia's countenance fell. She looked away and stuffed another strawberry into her mouth. "Sorry," she whispered under her breath.

Daphine tuned out the conversation. Her idea of a fun night did not consist of discussing murder over dinner.

"I'll be back," she said and disappeared before anyone could respond. She walked over to the window where the lights of the city twinkled like a concrete and glass universe. She leaned against the floor to ceiling windowpane until she spotted movement in her peripheral.

"I remember when this place wasn't so urban," an elderly man with graying blue eyes and a mole on his cheek said. He sat at a nearby table complaining to a woman who looked three decades younger than him.

The woman sipped her champagne and nodded. From the look in her eyes, she heard nothing he said, nor did she care about what she missed. She was there for his bank account not his personality.

"In my day, everyone knew their place," he droned on. "Certain types were not allowed in exclusive country clubs. Now, anyone can get into anywhere!"

His companion nodded and sipped, trying her best to look interested. If her mortgage wasn't past due, she would cut her losses and go home.

"Excuse me sweet cake, I have to go to the little boy's room," he said getting up from the table and slowly making his way across the room; a shadow followed close behind him.

Daphine put down her glass and followed behind him into the men's room.

The old man unzipped his pants and began to relieve himself when Daphine locked the door behind her and stood beside the urinal.

"What are you doing in here?" he growled zipping his trousers so fast that he almost zipped his most prized possession in the zipper.

"I overheard your conversation about how urban the club has become and some people not knowing their place. Who are these people?" she asked, leaning against the wall with her hand in her purse.

"He's talking about us," a voice whispered into Daphine's ear.

The old man scoffed; his eyes burning with fury.

"You don't have a right to ask me anything. You people have no boundaries. A man can't even piss in peace! Did affirmative action give you access to the toilet too?" he hissed.

"It's him," the voice said.

"No, it just gave me access to you," Daphine huffed as she pounced on the old man like a feral cat on a maimed squirrel. Her hand was out of her purse wielding a curved blade before he could move an inch.

The old man pushed her against the wall, but she was on his back before he could reach the door. Her blade dug deep into his pink flesh as his futile howl faded into a low gurgle. His body hit the floor. She tore open his button-down shirt and artfully engraved his left breast.

Daphine washed her hands and returned the blade to her purse. She rinsed off the bottom of her red-bottom heels and breathed a sigh of relief that she decided to wear all black. Bloodstains, if there were any, were not detectable on her dress. She took a paper towel and hand sanitizer and wiped her fingerprints from the door, then made her way back to the table to her friends.

"Where were you?" Zenobia asked loudly over the live band. "I took the liberty of ordering for you."

"Thanks. I appreciate that," Daphine said, her demeanor uneasy.

"You didn't tell me where you were," Zenobia prodded, her voice slurring a bit.

Two empty champagne glasses and one shot glass sat empty on the table next to Zenobia's purse.

Daphine laughed, "You can never hold your liquor. Sit back and stop breathing in my face."

Zenobia leaned away from her best friend and sighed, her head bobbing like an apple.

"Where did you go?" Zenobia asked, trying to contain her buzz. "You got something on your dress," she slurred reaching for a tiny bloody ball of flesh.

Daphine knocked her friend's hand away and quickly disposed of the human meat within her handbag.

"I thought I left my mama at home," Daphine quipped, unease creeping into her voice causing it to crack, then turned her attention towards Christavius. "Are you from Atlanta?"

"I am," he smiled. "Born and raised in East Lake Meadows."

"You from the hood!" Van laughed.

"So am I," Daphine replied. "I grew up in the West End. Harris Homes until..." her voice trailed off. Her glossy eyes fixed across the room.

"You better not cry!" a voice whispered into Daphine's ear.

"Until what?" Christavius asked, puzzled by Daphine's sudden pause and demeanor shift.

"Until her twin brother, Devante' got killed during the Atlanta Child Murders," Zenobia answered. "After then, she moved to Stone Mountain where we met in elementary school and been friends ever since."

"Oh my God! I'm sorry that happened to your brother," Christavius offered his condolences. "That was a scary time for all of us. I remember my parents not allowing my siblings and I to go outside to play and taking us to and from school instead of letting us walk like we used to. Rumors of children getting snatched on street corners and killers crawling through windows had us all shook. I can't imagine the trauma you suffered. Again, I'm so sorry for your loss."

Daphine diverted her eyes. Pools of mascara-tinged water accumulated and rolled down her cheeks.

"May I?" Christavius asked as he picked up a napkin.

Daphine nodded.

He gently wiped her face and folded the napkin into her hand then kissed it.

"I'm sorry," he whispered.

Daphine smiled at his kindness, took a deep breath, and pulled herself together.

"I like him," the voice whispered.

"Me too," she uttered a hushed reply.

"You too what?" Christavius asked, confused by her response. He placed his hand upon hers and waited.

"She too traumatized!" Zanobia belted, "Her brother getting' killed was especially traumatic for Daphine. She said she saw the kidnapper. She said he was a white man with gray-blue eyes and a mole on his face," Zenobia yelped, her breath smelling of champagne and strawberries.

"How many of these did you let her have?" Daphine asked Van who was busy stuffing his mouth with steak.

"She grown. I can't let her do nothin'," he mumbled while chewing.

Daphine was amazed that such a bony man could eat so much food.

"Chris, can you believe she date white men after she saw a white man kidnap her brother? He tried to kidnap her too, but she got away. Devante wasn't as lucky," Zenobia slurred, her hot breath blasting across the table. "They found his body days later behind the projects. Daphine ain't been right since."

"You doin' too much! I'm finna go!" Daphine barked angrily, picking up her purse and standing up. Her chair flew backwards and landed on its side with a booming thump. She couldn't believe Zenobia was so casually telling a stranger about her brother's death. Daphine wanted to strangle her, but before Daphine could storm away from the table, a team of police officers rushed into the ballroom.

"What's going on?" Van asked one of the servers who was trembling and crying hysterically. The woman pointed to the bathroom area.

"They found a dead man in the bathroom. Somebody killed him!"

+   +   +

Peaches' Pristine Porch, whose southern cuisine was praised throughout the south, was a black-owned landmark diner located on Auburn Ave next to the Royal Peacock "Club

Beautiful" – a famous Atlanta nightclub that hosted greats like Ray Charles, Marvin Gaye, and Martin Luther King, Jr. Now dancehall reggae and freestyle hip hop battles keep its doors ajar. Peaches' Pristine Porch was one of the first restaurants that openly served an integrated clientele without danger in the south and its walls still boasts of its activism promoting civil rights.

Daphine and Ms. Kat were escorted to a small table with a checkerboard tablecloth and white cloth napkins. A lone daffodil bobbled in a skinny crystal vase in the middle of the table.

"What time will your son get here?" Daphine asked, picking up a menu and flipping through the laminated pages edged with gold.

"I'm not sure. I haven't seen him. I've been calling him for days and he hasn't picked up. He left my house a week ago all dressed up with a young bimbo on his arm. It seemed clear to everyone but him that the only thing she was interested in was his wallet," Ms. Kat grumbled. "I figured he has been shacked up at her house for the week. I texted him a lunch reminder. He didn't reply, but he never misses a date."

"Maybe he's just running late," Daphine said, patting the back of Ms. Kat's hand to comfort her. A worried frown bent her lips as she sipped water with trembling hands.

An old retro black and white TV sat on the dessert counter.

"Can you turn that up for me please?" an older man, with a voice so smooth he could narrate documentaries, asked the waiter nicely.

Ms. Kat smiled at the man whose mahogany skin matched his plaid shirt and trousers.

"That's my kind of man," Ms. Kat meowed.

Daphine laughed so hard that her whole body submitted to hysteria.

"I don't know why he wants to watch the news. It's nothing but chaos and disorder. The news is banned from my house! I have no room for fearmongering," Ms. Kat spat.

"The newest victim of the A-town Massacres has been identified by his partner as Robert O'Hara, son of 109-year-old Atlanta socialite Katherine O'Hara. He was discovered in the restroom of an elite social club in Midtown Atlanta. Robert O'Hara was an engineer in his mid-seventies. The victim's partner said he was visiting family in the Atlanta area," Aashvi Patel reported through the black and white television.

Ms. Kat grabbed her chest and slid from her chair to the floor. By the time the ambulance arrived, she was cold.

+   +   +

"I didn't think our first date would end with us being questioned by the police about a murder," Christavius texted. "Redo?"

"Sure," Daphine texted back.

"I know it's short notice but are you busy tonight?" he texted.

Daphine closed a file on her desk and put it in a drawer. Her administrative assistant waved goodbye in the doorway and exited into the elevator.

Daphine leaned back in her chair and tried hard to think of a good excuse why she couldn't meet him. She could think of nothing, so she texted, "I'm free. What do you have in mind?"

"Meet me at Grant Park in the small pavilion. I'll be there at eight. I hope you like sushi," he texted.

"I don't." she replied. "I hate it in fact."

"Sweet tea pizza?" he texted.

"Now you're talking. ☺ See you soon." She texted and dropped her phone in her purse.

+   +   +

Daphine walked beneath the trees of Grant Park. Warm air tousled leaves and tickled the skin of her arms and face. She leaned against one of the trunks and slipped her sandals off and allowed her feet to sink into the plush emerald grass. She walked until she saw Christavius' wide smile shining from underneath the pavilion.

"Hey beautiful," he greeted, trotting to her and throwing his arms around her like they had known each other for decades.

Daphine uncomfortably reciprocated and forced a smile.

He slipped his arm inside hers and escorted her to a picnic table set with fine china and silverware. A bottle of expensive wine sat in the middle of the table with wine glasses decorated with flakes of gold and a sweet tea pizza as big as a car tire. A pair of electric candles flickered on each side of the entrée.

"Wow, all this for me?" Daphine laughed. She admired and appreciated his creativity. She sat down and dropped her belongings next to her. "The pizza smells so good. How did you keep it hot for so long?"

"I can't tell you my trade secrets," he joked as he slid into the seat across from her.

The couple laughed and talked for hours. Conversation flowed easily.

"It's getting dark. Want to continue this at my place?" Christavius smirked and placed his hand upon hers.

Daphine blushed. It had been a long time since she had entertained romance. Her life had no room for it.

"Let me think about it," she whispered. "I'm going to run to the bathroom real quick. I'll be right back."

Chris stood up.

"I'll walk you," he said.

"No need. I'll be back before you know it," she replied.

"But it's dark and the park can be dangerous at night. I would be more comfortable walking you," he insisted.

"I can take care of myself," she huffed, her eyes and brows pinching. She stood up from the table so quickly that she almost lost her balance.

"I know you can, but I wouldn't be a man if I didn't look after your safety," he replied trying not to chuckle. He found her fierce independence foolish but kind of sexy.

"You're right," she softened and exhaled. "Thank you for being a gentleman. Please escort me."

The couple walked to the stone lavatory building located near a fountain. Christavius watched Daphine enter the ladies' room then went into the men's room.

Daphine exited the bathroom stall with her purse in hand. She placed the purse strap on her shoulder and exited the restroom. The strap hooked onto the doorknob and snapped, spilling the contents in her purse onto the concrete. A combination of obscenities exited her mouth as she stooped down to pick up her things. As she gathered her belongings, a pair of pale hands handed her a tube of lipstick and her wallet.

"Here you go ma'am," a man said as he dropped the items into her hands.

Daphine surveyed his ivory face and studied his gray-blue eyes. Kindness rested there but that didn't matter. Age seemed to subjugate the wickedness of youth. A humble smile often hid the stain of past sins. A small flat mole rested on his cheekbone. His off-white tank top and biking shorts blended into his rosacea blotched skin.

She cocked her head to the side and spied his bicycle leaning against a tree. He handed her a package of tissues and her keys.

"I think this is it," he said. He turned on his cell phone's flashlight to ensure that there was nothing left to pick up. He extended his hand to help her up. She stood without assistance.

"Thank you," she said. Sweat began to dampen her armpits.

"You're welcome pretty lady. It was my pleasure," he smiled. "Make sure you hurry out of the park. It's getting pretty dark. There can be some unsavory people out at night," he warned as he turned and walked towards his bike.

"He is the unsavory one," a voice whispered to Daphine.

Daphine slipped her hands into the inner pocket of her purse and retrieved a pocketknife. Her eyes wild and stretched. Her teeth bared. Hot air pushing from her nostrils. She sprinted behind the friendly pedestrian and raised her knife above her head and drove it down between his shoulder blades with the strength of ten men. The blade slid through his back like a butterknife through a ripe strawberry. Blood splattered across her cheeks as she sliced life from the innocent. She turned the man onto his back and cut the front of his tank top open. She pressed her blade into his pectoral and began to inscribe her mark.

"Daphine!" Christavius screamed as he turned the corner.

Daphine looked up. Blood splattered across her face like raspberry jam.

"What are you doing!" Christavius yelped. His arms outreached. His eyes were affright. He took a step towards her.

"He...he...attacked me," she lied pulling her blade from the dead man leaking crimson at her feet. Daphine stood up and turned towards her date.

Christavius looked at the gnarled body then back at her. Except for the blood spattered across her face and clothes, she looked untouched. Not a hair was out of place. Not a wrinkle in her garments. Her makeup was flawless. Even her expression was serene.

He dialed 911 and put the phone on speaker.

"911. How can I help you?"

"A man has been stabbed in Grant Park. Please send help immediately. He's located near the public restrooms," Christavius said then hung up the phone, placed it into his pocket, then pulled out the gun resting in the small of his back.

"Tell me what happened," he whispered, his knuckles aching from his grip on the gun pressed against his thigh. "How did he attack you?"

Daphine's eyes alternated between his face and his gun.

"I was leaving the bathroom and he ran up on me," she whispered. "He rushed towards me, and I pulled a knife from my bag and stabbed him."

"What were you doing to his chest?" Christavius asked, anxiously tapping the barrel of the gun on his leg.

Daphine said nothing.

They locked eyes. Silence between them.

"Stab him," a voice whispered in her ear.

A small shadow darted in her peripheral.

Daphine's eyes followed the inky figure.

"If you stab him, you and I will finally be together," the shadow whispered as it stood behind Christavius.

Daphine leapt towards Christavius, knife overhead, face crazed. Christavius shot three bullets into her chest. She hit the ground in a twist of screams and cried. He rushed to her side. The shadow hovered over her dying face next to Christavius.

"Why?" Christavius asked as he kneeled and cradled her head in his arms. "Why?"

"He killed my brother," she gurgled, blood erupting from the sides of her mouth. "The man with the cold eyes and mole killed my brother. Every time I kill the man, he comes back, and I have to kill him again," she choked then looked past Christavius' tearing eyes into the face of the shadow. The inky black of the shadow faded into a technicolor being which shifted into the face of a light brown boy.

Sirens tore through the silence. Legions of footsteps rushed towards the bloody couple.

"Davante'," Daphine whispered; her eyes locked and staring in the distance. A smile bending her lips upward. Her chest stilled. Like her brother, she was gone.

Never Forget

Olusegun sprang up in the middle of the bed; chest heaving and heart pounding like the bata drums that haunted his dreams. Scorched air, hot and foul smelling filled his nose then vanished. Wiping the sweat from his ebony forehead with the back of his trembling hand, he exhaled.

The dream had come again. It was the seventh night in a row that he had seen the shadow descending upon him trying to swallow him whole. He looked over to his sleeping wife, Bunmi; relieved that he had not awakened her. Her insistent questioning would be another nightmare he didn't care to experience. Plus, he knew that his wife had to get up early in the morning for work. He didn't want to worry her.

Olusegun looked at the clock. It read 3:33 a.m.; the same time it had read all seven nights the dream had come. Thoughts of home nagged at him like an unreachable mosquito bite. Nigeria was calling him, but he was much too busy with his career and family to go back overseas. America was his home now. Decatur, Georgia is where he lived and where he intended to stay. No nightmare was going to drive him back home before he was good and ready to go.

Olusegun tossed his blanket to the side and got out of bed, making his way to the bathroom with lightning speed. He relieved himself then climbed back into bed next to his wife and forced his eyes closed. Sleep would not come, but that was okay. He would just lay there and meditate; quiet his mind and banish thoughts of home.

"Rise and shine," Bunmi kissed Olusegun on the forehead as she shook him softly. "It's time to get up!"

The smell of Bunmi's rose and honey scented hair drifted into his nose. He inhaled and smiled. Her lovely face was goddess-like; high cheekbones, almond shaped eyes, skin radiant and flawless like a black diamond.

Upon seeing Olusegun's eyes open and alert, Bunmi rushed out of their bedroom to wake their children. Full hips swinging like a pendulum, Bunmi's walk still had the ability to hypnotize him, making him drunk with admiration.

Within a half hour, the family of six sat at the breakfast table enjoying left over fried chicken and frozen waffles.

Kayode, the youngest boy, jumped from his seat and grabbed his lunch bag off the counter. He peaked inside and saw a sandwich, a bag of carrots, and a juice pouch. He twisted his mouth in disappointment and asked his mother, "Why can't I have chips instead of carrots?" he pouted.

"Carrots are better for you," she answered while rubbing her hands across his thick kinky hair.

"Kids at school have chips and they seem healthy to me!" he exclaimed.

"Those kids don't belong to me!" Bunmi yelped. "You do!"

"Adults know more sitting down than children know standing up," Olusegun interjected. "Take your lunch and go."

Kayode's frowned in surrender as he let out a disheartened sigh.

"Time for school," Bunmi said as she passed the other three children their lunches and kissed them on the way out the door; then, turned to her husband and wrapped her arms around his neck. "You haven't been sleeping," she whispered into his ear in an accent married to Alkebulan. "I'm concerned about you?"

"I'm okay," he lied, eyes ringed like a racoon.

"The dream again?" she asked.

"Yes, he admitted; his countenance falling. "Do not concern yourself with me. I will be okay. Go on to work."

"But, Olu…" her words were cut short by a kiss on the mouth.

"Go on. No more talking. You will be late," he opened the door and ushered her out. "Enjoy your day my love."

Bunmi reluctantly walked to her car as her husband turned off the light in the kitchen and went into his home office.

Writing code was like translating a novel to Olusegun; intricate poetry in a technological language few could understand. He tapped away on his laptop and sipped cold sorrel tea. His right hand continued to type as his left hand reached for his teacup. He mistakenly grabbed the cup by the rim, and the glass slipped from his fingertips shattering on the floor making a scarlet mess like a murder scene. He stood up with intentions to remedy the mess when the lights began to blink. Flashes of lightning filled the room like a plasma ball. A dark menacing figure appeared. Olusegun fell prostrate before the sneering man with eyes shining like the sun and skin blacker than a starless night. His red robes bellowed in the windless room.

"Why haven't you heeded my call?" the man asked; his voice thundering- a violent storm; his mouth turned downward in a vicious sneer.

"Who are you?" Olusegun cried out, burying his face in his hands.

"You know me!" the dark figure roared. "You know who I am!"

Olusegun dropped his hands and allowed his eyes to rest upon the face of the man. A burning sensation filled his chest. He had never seen the man before, but a strange familiarity lingered in the fissures of his memories.

"Remember who you are!" the being thundered, lightning flashing from his palms.

Yes, Olusegun knew him. The man was a part of him. A part of his people.

"Forgive me, Sango," Olusegun cried out shielding his eyes from the lightning shooting from Sango's body to and from the walls leaving scorch marks on the paint like Rorschach Test ink blots.

"Go home! Your mother is missing," Sango thundered, departing as quickly as he had come.

The temperature of the room returned to normal. The smell of melting paint tinged the air. How was he going to explain the damaged walls to Bunmi?

Olusegun dropped his arms and let out an audible sigh. He sat down at his computer and booked the first flight to Nigeria, picked up the phone, and told his wife why he must go. She scorned him for being superstitious and foolish. Bunmi reminded him that they had recently joined a church where they committed to leave all that primitive nonsense behind. She voiced her disapproval and displeasure but respected his decision to leave. He assured her that he would be back in a month or so and that he loved her more than anything.

It was late when Olusegun got off the plane in Abuja for a transfer flight to Ilorin. The wait was not long before he was up in the air again soaring over rivers and trees. Upon arrival, he rented a jeep and made his way to his childhood home.

A small house sat upon a hill surrounded by trees and frolicking animals. He got out of his jeep and walked down a dirt path which led to a wooden porch filled from end to end with empty chairs. Olusegun knocked three times on the door and waited. He didn't expect the door to open because Sango said that the old woman was gone. Olusegun grabbed the knob with one hand and used his body weight to push against the door. The door opened and Olusegun stumbled forward almost knocking over a heavy-set woman, with thick gray hair, standing over the threshold. Her eyes looked distant and intoxicated.

"Olusegun," she mumbled in a monotone voice; looking through him as if he was an apparition.

"Iya," he called, confused by her zombified condition and her presence at the house. His mother was a teetotaler. She had never touched alcohol a day in her life. For her to be swaying like a palm tree was strange indeed. "Iya, what's wrong with you?"

"The jinn," she slurred.

"What do you mean?" he inquired as her eyes glazed over.

"It has taken a hold on the village. It has come to swallow our ethos and spit us out! It has taken the children" she mumbled.

"Taken them where?" he asked.

"To the river to die," she replied staring off.

"How did this happen?" Olusegun questioned, confused about how the children of Sango were overtaken by a jinni.

"Gathered them into the schoolhouse," she mumbled.

"Who gathered them?" he asked.

"When you left, the missionaries came," she whispered like there was someone there besides the two of them.

"What does missionaries have to do with jinn?" he asked.

"Charlatans tricked the children. Filled them with lies. Took away who they were. Called them children of the devil. Converted. Forbade worship. Took what they wanted, and then left them confused and empty. Empty vessels must be filled. In came the jinn. It had been waiting for eons to have the children. The missionaries coming and going gave it a way in. The children went from bad to worse. Abandoned their ancestors and Sango's protection. They don't know who they are. They mimic the monsters who misled them..." her words trailed off as she fainted into his arms.

Olusegun caught her before she hit the porch floor and carried her into the house. He laid her on an old sofa covered with patched blankets. The small house was warm and rudimentary. Furniture was sparse. Thin curtains hung in the windows. There was no air conditioning, but a few oscillating fans humming in the warm room.

Sango's altar laid on its side in the corner of the room; the desecrated altar's offerings spread across the floor like trash. The smell of ash filled the room. The holy books of foreigners sat on a small table near the altar.

Olusegun quickly put the altar upright and placed the offerings back on it. A double axe sat in the middle of the table surrounded by cedar tools, apples, rum, and amala -a cornmeal porridge made with okra. After cleaning up and restoring the altar, he picked up a bata drum and began to play.

The room grew warm, then hot, then sweltering. Fat drops of sweat rolled down Olusegun's face as he tried to gather the words to say. It had been decades since he had uttered a prayer to Sango. Olusegun truly didn't know how to ask for protection and the power to rescue the children. The smell of desperation mingled with fear filled the room as Olusegun sang and danced around the room. His drum like the very heartbeat of God permeating everything with its power. A bolt of lightning came through the window and struck Olusegun knocking him across the room. His dark skin glowed in crimson; his eyes were balls of fire; his fingertips pulsating flames.

A great wind blew the door open and knocked down every lightweight piece of furniture in the house including the altar. Olusegun was thrown against a wall. He quickly regained his footing. His mother was knocked off the sofa and pushed into a corner where she wept bitterly.

In the doorway, stood a giant, skin as bronze as an Egyptian's, dressed in Arabian garb. A golden turban wrapped his raven hair. A teal vest covered his massive chest. His torso ended in a swirling tornado that glistened with sand and sun.

"You are not welcome here!" the jinn roared, his sand-colored eyes flashing. "Go back home!"

"This is my home," Olusegun thundered back in the voice of Sango.

The jinn's thundering laugh echoed through the house.

"You left this place behind long ago. It is not yours to claim. The children are mine. They know nothing of you! In your heart you held the chronicles of your ancestors. Elders passed the torch to you! When the opportunity for a new life emerged, you left without passing it on. You abandoned your position. Through the lack of knowledge, the children will perish!" the jinn said as his swirling tail carried him into the home. "Now they are mine!"

"I went to school…" Olusegun said in his own voice, the voice of Sango trembling beneath it like an inharmonious whisper.

"You never came back! They are mine!" the jinn howled.

Olusegun dropped his head. The power of Sango pulsating in him began to fade.

The jinn laughed again, this time causing Olusegun's mother to let out a horrifying scream as the jinn hovered over her trembling body then vanished.

Olusegun rushed to his mother's side and helped her back onto the sofa.

"What can I do Iya?" he asked while cleaning the blood from the small scratches on her knees.

"You are home," his mother muttered, "put home back in the hearts of the children," she whimpered and fainted.

Olusegun shook her shoulders, but she continued to sleep. Pacing the room, he tried to decipher what purpose he could serve amid the unholy war he found himself pulled into. What could he possibly do with a jinni? Why was he called by Sango back to Nigeria? Surely there was someone better suited to free the village children from the jinn. Olusegun had no power. His westernized education facilitated the shunning of his traditions at a young age. He knew very little of the old ways; only the Yoruba language that his mother forced him to speak when she communicated with him.

Hours passed and Olusegun was still pacing the floor, his circular striding now back and forth in a straight line. His eyes rested upon his mother's still form lying on the sofa; watching her body rise and fall with each breath like a gigantic pulsating heart hanging outside its cushioned chest.

His eyes then found Sango's altar scattered and dismantled in the corner of the room. Olusegun made his way to the desecrated mess and swiftly put it back in order. The holy books of foreigners, he tossed out of the window. Oppression and colonization went with them.

He picked up the drum again, this time pausing before playing. Conjuring the jinn again was not an option, but he knew he needed to beat the drum, and summon the orisha that sanctified it to save the children; but how? Olusegun began to pace again. Sweat flowed down his temples into the corners of his eyes burning them with their salt. Thoughts of those long gone filled his mind; remembrances of his great grandfather teaching him how to cultivate the earth and hunt for sustenance came followed by images of his aunts teaching him to heal with plants and powders and his grandmother speaking in the native tongue of his people telling him about the infinite power of Olodumare who brought everything into being. He heard uncles strategize war and cousins tell stories of the heroes of old. Ancestors of blood and of brotherhood and sisterhood imbued every centimeter of his mind with aboriginal knowledge.

Olusegun began to play the drum. He opened his mouth and sang in the tongue of his people. His hips and arms spun as his back jerked to the holy rhythm forged by his hands and heart. Frenzied and full of spirit, he found himself before the altar. He froze and inhaled the power of all who had lived before him. Olusegun picked up Sango's hammer and headed to the river.

Like zombies, the children hobbled around the river, eyes blank and staring. Some children's beautiful earthtone skin was bleached and blotched. Some were stomping upon the ceremonial garments of their ancestors. Some were wearing strange wigs to hide their cottony coils. Some were hypnotized by images pulsating through cellphones. Some were pointing weapons at sisters and brothers mistaking family for foes. Some were gouging on chemicalized food planting cancer in their flesh. Like zombies, the children hobbled, eyes and mind blank and headed for cultural death.

Olusegun fell to his knees and cried out, seeing his children's faces in their faces.

"Sango, fill me!" Olusegun screamed.

Lightning struck the top of his head. He cried out. His voice, the sound of thunder shaking the children from their stupor. Olusegun roared and the children fell to their knees. He thundered, his voice infiltrating their souls, filling their hearts with the history of their people.

Winds gathered from the four corners of the earth, sucking the children into a tornado. Their cries rang through the air like a death knell. Standing face to face with Olusegun, the jinn appeared, its eyes vicious and its vengeance hungry. With a wave of one of its' hands, the children were tossed into the river. The water swallowed them in one gulp like a greedy baby.

"Oya, my love," Sango sang from Olusegun's mouth. "My river queen, give them back to me. Blow your fierce winds and birth the children from your waters my love. They are our children. Set them free! They carry our immortality in their hearts."

The waters of the river churned, and the children were spat upon the shore like peppercorns from a salivating maw. Out of the waves rose a being as terrible as she was beautiful. Red and purple robes wrapped around her black skin in bellowing storm clouds. A rainbow crowned her braided mane. A golden necklace with a diamond buffalo hung around her neck.

"Where are you, my love?" she whispered into Olusegun's mind.

Olusegun fell to his knees and thunder echoed from his throat. Billions of lightning bolts shot from his mouth and formed a towering creature beside him. Sango stepped forward and Olusegun fell to his side and wept.

"I am here, wife," Sango sang, smoke and fire drifting from his mouth. "Shall we, my queen?" he asked, extending his hand for her to take. Oyo's long fingers wrapped around his as she stepped onto the shore.

The jinn's lower body began to swirl into a psychotic cyclone, leveling everything in its path.

Olusegun gathered the children around him. He whispered to them about the orisha's that came to their defense. He told them about the ancestors who worked on their behalf. The children began to sing. As their voices lifted up into the heavens, Oyo and Sango spun in cyclones like the jinn. As the children sang, their voices combined with the voices of their ancestors into an ethereal choir. As they sang, the winds and the waves became weapons in the hands of Oyo as lightning and fire blasted from the palms of Sango. The children sang as the jinn was captured and bound in chains of fire and water and drug down by grabbing waves within the gaping mouth of the Niger.

Oyo and Sango kissed deeply, then disappeared into the damp afternoon breeze.

"Go home," Olusegun told the children. "And never forget who you are."

The children ran off to their homes as Olusegun made his way back to his mother. When he neared her house, he saw her standing, waiting, smiling in the doorway as plump and healthy as ever.

"Iya!" Olusegun cried as he ran to her and wrapped his arms around her. He spun her around and sat her down clumsily.

"The children?" his mother asked, half smiling half crying.

"The children are home," he answered, "and home is in them."

"You have done well," she kissed his face and hugged him tight.

Olusegun spent an additional week with his mother remembering and venerating the old ways before he took a flight home to Atlanta. When he opened the door to his house, Bunmi and their four children rushed to him and covered his face with kisses and hugs.

"We've missed you so much!" Bunmi cried. "When you were gone, I dreamed constantly of lightning and water. I dreamed of Oyo," her voice trailed off. For the first time in a long time, she remembered the history her grandmother taught her.

He grabbed his wife by the shoulders and gathered his children into his arms.

"We must never forget," he cried. "We must teach the children to never forget."

The Sisters of Drewberry

Drewberry, Georgia was a small town; population two hundred and fifty-seven. Named after its founder Cleophus Leroy Drewberry Jr., a mild mannered but fiercely passionate farmer who loved his wife so much that he gave her a baby for every year of their marriage. Cleophus fathered thirty-nine children and his twenty-five sons, and fourteen daughters fathered a small nation themselves. Rumor had it that all the residents of the town were related in some way or another.

Drewberry sat near a small manmade lake shaped like a porkchop. The towns people affectionately called the lake "Pork Juice" in honor of the lake's odd shape and the bacon-like scent that drifted off the water.

On one side of Pork Juice was a bright blue shanty house and on the other was a pea green one. In the blue shack lived the town healer, Lula Bell Drewberry, and in the green shack lived her identical twin sister, the town witch, Lola Mae Drewberry. Truly identical, the eighty-year-old twins were the same weight, same height, had the same fashion sense, the same tone of voice, the same sepia skin; even the chocolate chip shaped moles on their noses were the same except that Lula's mole was on her right nostril and Lola's mole was on her left.

The feuding sisters would never be caught dead on the opposite sides of the lake. Whispers said that they were once inseparable until they both fell in love with the same man, Irwin Garrett, sixty years ago.

Irwin Garret was an island man. He appeared one day out of nowhere at the local train station, where Lula and Lola worked, with his shirt tossed over his shoulder and sweat running down his face onto his broad, hairy chest. He was the biggest, tallest, widest man they had ever seen; pure, hard muscle.

"That's what Sampson in 'da Bible musta looked like," Lola sang in her thick southern drawl.

"Uh uh. A man like that must look like Jesus!" Lula drooled. "Only the son of Gawd could look that good." She slurped up her drool and sighed.

Lola tapped Lula's chin closing her gaping mouth.

Irwin instantly hypnotized the sisters with his smooth Caribbean accent, his strong bowlegs, his dashing white smile, his thick kinky hair, and his coal black skin. Never had Lula and Lola seen a man so beautiful. From the moment they laid eyes on him, the competition began. They rushed to the man's house with casseroles, cakes, and pies; each sister stuffing his mouth with edibles; trying to best the other. Rumors said he gained fifteen pounds in the three months that he resided in Drewberry.

Each one of the twins took him for walks on alternate days in hopes of persuading him to pick one or the other. But, instead of picking, he decided to take both, unbeknownst to the ladies of course. He told Lola that she was his soulmate and told Lula that she was the most beautiful woman in the world. He told Lola that he only had eyes for her and told Lula that she was the only woman for him. Eventually Irwin talked so much that he talked them both out of their clothes; marrying both of them secretly in faux ceremonies performed by a bootlegger posing as a preacher. The ladies were sworn to secrecy. Blissful and self-satisfied, they waived at each other across Pork Juice, each thinking they had won the heart of Irwin. Of course, he had convinced them to stay in their own houses and not to visit the other because he did not want to cause a rift between the sisters. Everything was gravy until both twins were expecting twins.

One day as Lola and Lula sat on their porches on the opposite sides of Pork Juice, Lula noticed how plump Lola had become. Lola was as round bellied as Lula was; so, Lula marched, knees tapping her protruding belly, out of her yard, around Pork Juice and straight down the path to Lola's front porch.

"Why you so fat all of a sudden? Whatchu been eatin'? Lula asked curiously with one hand on her hip and the other fingering a gold locket that Irwin had given her.

"Nothin' but the sweet kisses of my man," Lola purred. "Come here and sit down," she invited her sister onto the porch. A heavily cushioned rocking chair was waiting to be sat in.

Lula wobbled onto the porch and sat in the rocking chair next to her sister. Cat bones were scattered on the table between them.

"I see you still divining and dealing in devilment," Lula laughed.

Lola smiled as she picked up the cat bones and put them in her apron pocket. The gold locket around her neck swinging with every movement.

"You talkin' 'bout me, you kinda full looking yourself. Whatchu been eating?" Lola asked, eying her sister's round tummy.

"I have a secret," Lula said, smiling so hard that her lips touched her ears.

"What girl?" Lola asked clapping her hands and jumping up and down like a girl of ten. "I got one too! You go first then I'll tell you mine."

"I'm pregnant!" Lula exclaimed.

"Congratulations!" Lola cried. "Me too!"

"Who da' daddy?" Lula asked, joyously.

"My husband Irwin! Who else!" Lola replied.

Lula's face melted like lard in a cast iron pan. "Irwin who?" she asked, rolling her neck, and raising one of her brows; a look that would've frightened away Death on her face.

"Irwin Garret. Who else?" Lola grinned as she held up her hand to show her sister a ring with a diamond as big as a grain of sugar.

"That's my man!" Lula wailed showing her sister an identical ring squeezing her swollen finger.

Two soul wrenching screams echoed through Drewberry until they coaxed thunder from the clouds.

"You slept with my husband!" Lula screamed.

"You a fool! He's my husband. Pastor Crooklyn married us in the woods last Easter," Lola yelled back, spit spraying her sisters face.

Lula wiped her face with the back of her hand and barked, "That's impossible! Irwin was out of town visiting his mama last Easter. He married me the weekend after he returned from the trip!"

On and on the twins argued into the wee hours of the night. They blamed each other instead of the culprit that invaded both their temples. Lula accused Lola of concocting a spell to steal her man and Lola accused Lula of making him drunk with peach brandy and tricking him into marrying her. Of course, Irwin Garret had left town the day their screams brought down the thunder never to be seen again.

That very day, the sisters parted ways and never exchanged a kind word with each other again. Their identical children grew up on opposite sides of the lake, forbidden to speak to their identical cousins. Sixty years passed and their anger burned as hot as ever.

The only time the sisters were in the same vicinity was on Drewberry Day, a local festival where the town's people gathered to show off their crafts, listen to live music, shop the local merchants, and watch the sisters engage in their annual battle to determine which one was the most powerful.

It was Drewberry Day, and the entire town was abuzz with excitement. The sound of a wooden stage being constructed, vendor tables being dragged and dropped in their proper locations, hanging of banners being flung on poles, and balloons popping echoed through the small town.

Lola marched around her house mumbling and cursing as she gathered her good luck sprays and protection satchels, her divining tools and tarot cards, her candles and cat bones to load into her cart for the Drewberry volunteers to pick up and set up.

Across Pork Juice, Lula shuffled through cabinets and grumbled to herself as she gathered balms and creams, herbs and salves, tinctures and powders into large baskets for the upcoming event. Volunteers waited patiently outside her door ready to collect her items and carry them to her booth.

Within an hour, music floated through the city on rhythmic wings of blues, jazz, rock and roll, and African drumming. Fried pies, barbeque, and lemonade glazed the lips of Drewberry citizens as they tossed rings around bottles to win stuffed animals and yelled lighthearted threats while engrossed in spades tournaments. Tents selling everything from handmade candles and jewelry to figurines made in China lined the edges of Pork Juice like the crunchy crust of a perfectly fried porkchop.

The biggest tents stood side by side: a pink one housing Lula and a purple housing

Lola. Equally long lines of fidgeting people formed in front of each tent. Clients paying top dollar for Lula's healing ointments, arthritis treatments, cough syrups, and weight loss teas waited patiently next to Lula's customers hoping to get dream interpretations, lottery numbers, love spells, and good luck sprays. Like a folk factory assembly line, the sisters served their specialties to grateful Drewberrians with the speed of a twelve man work crew. Just when the twins thought they had served their last customer an old woman stood right in the middle of both tents.

"How can I help you?" the sisters said in unison. Instantly rolling their eyes at the other.

"She's in my line," Lola snapped, waving the woman towards her tent. "I had a dream about you last night. I have a message for you in my spirit. There's something real different about you." Lola's eyes ran over the woman who was dressed from head to toe in black. An antique gold heart-shaped locket hung around the woman's neck identical to the lockets dangling from the necks of the twins. Lola's brow raised.

"That nice woman don't want none of your snake oil! The only thing you dream about is my egg pie and collard greens because you know you ain't gone never taste them again,"

Lula retorted then turned to the woman. "Honey, I got something for that stiff knee of yours."

"Thank God for that!" Lola spat. "Your food is as nasty as yo' feet! Your toenails look like a pile of pork rinds."

Lula's comeback, "Your molely back looks like a chocolate chip cookie!"

"Shut up you decrepit old hag!" Lola grumbled while eyeballing the stranger's locket.

"Ladies," the old woman laughed. She lifted her hand to squash their spat. "My name is Magnolia. Magnolia Garrett, and I came to see the both of you."

The twins looked at one another in shock then back at the elderly stranger.

Magnolia was short and brown just like them. Her features were so familiar that she could have passed for their sister.

"You must not be from around here," Lola stated with arms crossed and lips pursed. "Everyone in Drewberry knows that me and that thang over there," she said pointing to her sister. "don't commune. If you want to talk to us, you need to make separate appointments."

Lula nodded; the first time the sisters had agreed in six decades.

"I'm not. I'm from the town over. Last week I met four middle-aged men, about the same age as my son and the spitting image of my late husband," Magnolia said. "They told me that ya'll were their mamas. Such handsome men. My son doesn't know any of my husband's people. I figured with the resemblance; our sons must be pretty close cousins."

The sisters looked at each other again and crossed their arms in a synchronized motion. After all they had done to keep their sons apart, they found a way to each other. The twins wondered how long the cousins had been fraternizing. They also wondered about Magnolia's son and how he was related to their boys. Irwin's people were a mystery to them too.

"Look at her necklace," Lola whispered to Lula. Lula's eyes stretched then narrowed into indignant slits.

"Where did you get that locket?" Lula asked, her voice sharp and cutting like the edge of a broken liquor bottle.

"From my Irwin of course," the stranger smiled and stroked the gold heart.

"Lemme see that," Lola barked as she closed in on Magnolia with one big step and pulled the locket upward almost yanking the old woman's neck off her shoulders. Lola flipped the locket open with her thumb. She gasped as Irwin's grinning eyes looked up at her from the gold casing.

"That dirty dawg!" she yelped, pulling the necklace so her sister could see it; almost causing the gold chain to cut through Magnolia's neck.

"That's my husband!" Lula cried.

"Mine too!" Lola squealed.

Magnolia snatched her locket free of the twin's boney hands and stepped backwards without losing her footing.

The twins opened their lockets showing Magnolia the same asinine photo of Irwin grinning, eyes and teeth whiter than aspirin.

Magnolia swooned and staggered but was too much of a lady to fall to the ground and dirty up her freshly pressed hair and crisp starched suit.

"He's going to answer for this!" Lula screeched.

"He's dead," Magnolia simpered while holding her chest and perspiring heavily. "The good Lord took him years ago."

Lula grabbed a cup of tea from her booth and handed it to Magnolia.

"Drink this. It'll calm your nerves," she said.

Magnolia sipped the tea and sat on the edge of one of Lula's dried flower barrels.

Lola dragged a table and three chairs from behind her booth. She placed a candle, a mirror, a pendulum, and a few objects on the table. She placed the chairs around the table and instructed Magnolia and Lula to sit down.

"It's better with four or more people but we'll work with what we got," Lola said as she plopped down in a chair.

"What are you doing?" Lula asked, giving her sister the side eye.

"I'm finna make that scoundrel explain himself," Lola replied.

"Oh no!" Magnolia objected as she stood up and backed away from the table. "I plead the blood of Jesus over the spirit of witchcraft!"

Lola rolled her eyes and said, "Plead the blood of Jesus right there in that seat and don't get up again or you'll break the circle."

Magnolia declined the invitation to the chair. She pulled a small bible from her purse and did the sign of the cross over her head and chest.

"Suit yourself. When Irwin shows up, I ain't gone let you speak to him," Lola said as she arranged the items on the table just how she wanted them.

Magnolia slowly sat down, whispering Psalm 91 under her breath so the Lord would protect her from this devilment.

The three held hands as Lola lit the candle and said a few obscure words and fiddled around as she called Irwin up from the grave. After a few minutes, fog clouded the mirror. Little by little, Irwin's face materialized, a faded replica of his former self.

"Hey baby," he exclaimed, his smile broad and charming. "I've missed you, Lola."

A tear rolled down Lola's cheek. He looked like he did the last time she had laid eyes on him.

"Did you miss us too?" Lula and Magnolia peaked into the looking glass, both angrier than a turkey in November and more annoyed than a mastermind tracing the alphabet.

Irwin's smile turned upside down. "L..L..L..ladies I...I...I," he stuttered so badly nothing he uttered was understandable.

"You're a dang gone clown!" Lola spat. "Since you like ladies so much, you gone spend the rest of eternity with them!"

Lola mumbled, sprinkled and spat. A multitude of faces appeared behind Irwin. Ghastly women—haints and hags, hissing and howling, pulled and gnawed at every inch of

Irwin Garrett, molesting him with gnarled fingers and rotting lips. His baritone voice boomed so loudly that the mirror fell from the table and shattered.

"I'm sorry," Lula cried as she jumped up from the table and threw her arms around her sister.

"I'm sorry too," Lola wept as she buried her face in Lula's shoulder; their sixty-year feud finished like Irwin Garrett.

Gallons of tears ran down Magnolia's face. She hopped up from the table and put her arms around the both of them. "I'm sorry too," Magnolia wailed.

"What are you sorry for?" the sisters laughed, sniffling, and welcoming her into the fold.

"That we didn't catch that rascal sooner."

Goldie and the Bears

"It was a Wednesday. No, a Thursday. It had to be a Thursday because I had just left my twerk fitness class and I only do that class on Thursday afternoons. I distinctly remember being hyped because the class had gotten a new instructor, and she was simply dynamite! She had us winding our hips like we were from the motherland. I felt so energetic after working out that I decided to walk home instead of calling for a rideshare.

What a beautiful fall day! The autumn leaves lit the sides of the sidewalk on fire as I strolled down the road. Enjoying the weather so much, I became hypnotized by the whistling of the wind, the dancing of the leaves, and the buzzing of nearby insects. Nature had me in a trance. I missed my turn and ended up on an unfamiliar street. I thought I knew my neighborhood like the back of my hand, but I had never been on that street before. Instead of row houses, there were three small cottages lined up on one side of the street facing what looked like a vast forest on the other. Puzzled, I began to explore. Never in a million years did I think I could become lost in my own darn neighborhood."

"Is this when you ran into them?" the older woman asked, her skin blending into the leather chair like a monochromatic creature in camouflage.

"No. I didn't meet them until later on that night."

The older woman raised her brow and said, "Please proceed."

"I was being nosey, so I walked up to the cottages and peeked into the windows. All the cottages were fully furnished but seemed unoccupied. I wondered if they were the products of new construction. New construction was happening everywhere in the city. Our population has tripled in the last decade."

"How does that make you feel?" asked the older woman.

"I feel that the town I grew up in is changing so drastically that it hardly feels like home. Not that I don't welcome change; it's all just happening so quickly. Everything is so different. I don't even recognize the neighborhood I grew up in!"

The older woman replied, "Change can be hard, but you seem like the type of woman who welcomes change. Your dreadlocks for instance; they are dyed such a dynamic shade of gold. When you first came in, your clothes were brightly colored with various patterns. Your nose was pierced and so was your belly button. I remember you telling me that you worked in healthcare, and you cared deeply for your community and their having access to resources that helped promote positive change," said the older woman.

"Very true, but change over time, not instantly, is easier to digest."

The older woman nodded and said, "Tell me more about the new neighborhood."

"It was lovely. It reminded me of the pictures I used to see in the Mother Goose nursery rhyme book I had as a child. The cottages were brightly colored with flower gardens so lushly patterned that they looked like edible arrangements. I was tempted to take a bite out of a flower that looked like a giant lollipop.

As I walked up to the third house, I inhaled the most delicious scent. It smelled like oatmeal cookies dipped in honey. My stomach started to growl so loudly that I looked over my shoulder to make sure it was me making all that noise. As I walked up the walkway to the porch, that smell became more potent. Before I knew it, I started trotting to the door. An enormous swing was suspended from the porch ceiling on one side of the front door and a massive wicker table with three chairs sat on the other dwarfing me like a human foot to an ant. I felt like golden-egg-stealing-Jack at the portico of the giant's home. The table was as high as my chest and the chairs my stomach. I peeked inside of a large window. No one was there. I knocked on the front door and waited. Snaking itself into my nostrils, the sweet aroma drove me into a frenzy. I never wanted anything so badly in my life! I knocked again, harder, and relentlessly. The side of my fist became tender. My pinky knuckle ached against the wood. No one answered. For a moment, I stopped pounding and began to pace. Obviously, there was no one home, but I needed to get inside. That delectable smell drove me to the edge of madness. I banged one more time. Nothing. Tears rolled down my face. Frustration filled me. I tried the knob and it opened with a tiny squeak. My anxiety dissipated immediately."

"Do you walk into stranger's homes often?" the older woman asked. "That's a blatant invasion of privacy."

"Never! I had never done anything like that before. It was something about that smell that made me open that door. I had to have whatever was cooking!"

The older woman raised one eyebrow.

"I know it sounds crazy and impulsive, but I had to open the door and enter the cottage. I just had to, so I did," the woman snapped, attempting to justify her behavior. "I yelled hello, no one answered, so I followed my nose to the kitchen. Like outside, the furniture inside was just as massive. I rose up on my toes. On the table were three frosted glass bowls with flecks of gold filled with what looked like oatmeal, or some type of porridge covered in honey, butter, and maybe a sprinkle of cinnamon. I climbed onto the largest chair like a clumsy toddler and took a taste out of the first bowl. The food burned my mouth. I dropped the spoon and howled. I could have sworn my tongue blistered under the heat. I cursed myself for being so stupid and attempted to walk out of the house, but the smell wooed me back into the kitchen. I tried the second bowl. This time, being proactive, I blew the food to ensure that my mouth would not catch fire a second time. I placed the spoon to my tongue, and it was ice cold. I spat the slimy gruel on the floor to prevent myself from vomiting. The taste was atrocious!"

"You spat on their floor?" the older woman asked with a judgmental sigh. "You invade private property, and you defile it.

Interesting. That's an inappropriate sense of entitlement."

"Shamefully, yes, but I cleaned it up with a paper towel."

The older woman respired loudly like she was pushing something thick from her lungs, concerned with the woman's lack of accountability. "Please continue."

"Again, I tried to leave but that heavenly aroma pulled me back into the kitchen. I closed my eyes and dug into the third bowl. It tasted like manna from heaven. Never had something so divine entered my mouth. One spoon turned into ten and then the entire bowl was empty. I scraped the sides of the bowl with my spoon and even licked the rim of the bowl. Euphoria filled me. My head swam lightly. My root chakra pulsating, I gasped in pleasure. I don't know what they put in that stuff, but I wanted more. I tried to go back to the other bowls, but they remained too hot or too cold to consume. My euphoria heightened. My knees became weak. I stumbled into the living room and sat on a large recliner. It felt like sitting on a slab of marble. I moved to the lush velvet chair next to it, sat down and sank to the bottom of it like an anchor in the ocean. Lush pillows swallowed me whole. It took me fifteen minutes to climb out of its cushiony mouth onto the floor. After I regained my footing, I pulled myself onto the most comfortable chair I had ever sat in. I leaned back and allowed myself to melt into its firm comfort. I had only closed my eyes for a second before my solace was ripped from me by the chair beneath me crashing to the floor. I'm not a small woman, but I'm not heavy enough to break a chair!"

The older woman smirked at the remark but said nothing.

"I got up from the rubbish. My head was swimming. Suddenly, I felt sleepy, so I climbed the stairs to find somewhere to lay."

"You were very comfortable in an unfamiliar house," the older woman observed. "You ate food, broke furniture, and now you wanted to sleep."

"Yes, I must admit I was."

"Do you always feel entitled to other people's belongings?" asked the older woman. She crossed her muscled legs and adjusted herself in her seat for better comfort.

"No, but I was really sleepy. Sleepier than I had ever been. I could hardly keep my eyes open as I climbed the stairs. Maybe the porridge was drugged. I don't know. I just knew I needed to sleep. Sluggish and groggy, I made it to the second floor. There were two doors up there: both hard wood with ornate carvings of leaves falling down the middle of the doors. I opened the first door and stepped into a strangely furnished room."

"What made it strange?" the older woman asked.

"There were two full sized beds in the middle of the room, kinda like a hotel."

The older woman nodded.

"I stumbled to the first bed and plopped down. My ribs stung from the impact. That bed felt like a pile of bricks! I rolled onto the floor, holding my side, and crawled to the next bed. I pulled myself up and climbed upon it, sinking into the mattress like quicksand. I fought to catch my breath as I flailed madly to get free from the bed. Somehow, God didn't see fit for my life to end in a cushioned hell, I was able to grab the edge of the headboard and pull myself free."

"That's one soft bed," said the older woman under her breath.

"You tellin' me!"

The older woman chuckled. "What happened next?"

"I made my way to the other room and climbed into the queen-sized bed sitting in the middle of the floor. I was sleep before my head hit the pillow."

"Comfy huh?" asked the older woman.

"It felt so good that it felt sinful. I don't know how long I slept. When I opened my eyes, there was moonlight pouring into the window and that oatmeal smell was replaced by something savory and fishy."

"Interesting," the older woman said. "What happened next?

"I rolled over and fell asleep again. The bed was too comfortable to get out of. I felt trapped by its comfort!"

"Did you sleep there until morning?" the older woman asked while scribbling on her tablet.

"A loud roar followed by a symphony of growls snatched me from my sleep. I opened my eyes to three maws full of sharp, drool-dripping teeth and three sets of demonic eyes surveying my body like lasers ready to fire!" the woman yelped, adjusting in her seat as if the monstrous jaws were still before her. "Three beasts! One bigger than the next leaned over me, claws curved and ready to slice, as I scrambled to the furthest corner of the bed. I screamed but no sound came. At that moment, I knew I was going to die when the most peculiar thing happened."

"What happened?"

"The beast spoke," the golden-haired woman whispered. "The smallest one asked, its voice distressed and childlike, 'Who are you? Why are you sleeping in my bed?"

The older woman scribbled on her tablet and nodded silently.

"I couldn't believe my ears. Its voice soft and sweet like cotton candy; the antithesis of what I imagined would come out of its menacing mouth. The cub hovered over me; its nose almost touching mine; its furry face like the dark side of the moon," she yelped.

"The bear talked? Interesting," the older woman scribbled. "Your story sounds oddly familiar."

The woman frowned. She knew her story sounded like an old fairytale, but that didn't make it untrue.

"Please continue," the older woman requested, uncrossing her legs and pouring herself a glass of water from a crystal carafe. "What happened next?"

"I told the baby bear I was tired!" the woman snapped.

The older woman pierced her lips to keep from smiling.

"Well, I was!" She rolled her eyes and crossed her arms.

The older woman nodded, urging her to continue.

"My answer upset the baby bear. It cried, a blubbering mess, then turned to its mother and clung to her hairy thigh as if I attacked it! Seeing the baby bear weep infuriated the mother. Her eyes burned into my face; a hungry growl blew from her mouth like a gust of foul-smelling wind blowing my locs behind my shoulders. I clung to the pillows and braced myself to be eaten alive. The biggest bear stepped in front of the mother and child. Tall, dark with broad shoulders and a powerful presence, it was fearsome but attractive for a bear."

"Attractive for a bear?" the older woman asked, befuddled by the woman's assessment of the animal.

"I know. I know!" the woman rolled her eyes. "You had to see it."

The older woman scribbled on her tablet. She asked the woman to continue.

"The biggest bear yelled, 'Get out!' Its maw snapping. Its eyes dangerous. It's chest heaving. I imagined my head between its jaws, my skull popping like a cherry tomato. It didn't have to tell me twice to leave. I hopped out of bed. I felt hands all over me; paws enclosing my writhing limbs. I broke free and ran for my life! I ran and ran until I arrived here!" she exclaimed, breathless, flurried. "I've never run so fast in all my life."

"Why is that lady talking to herself in the mirror?" a young nurse intern asked, carrying a tray of medications in tiny plastic cups. "I heard she used to be a doctor here."

"That's Dr. Goldie Brooks. She used to be one of our best psychiatrists. She's processing a heartbreak," the Director of Nursing answered. "She thinks she's helping a patient, but she's just talking to herself in the mirror.

"What happened?" the intern inquired watching the doctor interrogate her reflection.

"Dr. Goldie fell in love with a married man named Barrington Forrest. He was a sales rep that frequented our psychiatric clinic. Charming and charismatic, he always brought us gifts. We loved it when he brought these organic oatmeal and honey candles. His wife owned a shop downtown. Those candles were incredible. They were packaged in beautiful, frosted glass tied with a gold satin ribbon. The wax itself was infused with 24k gold flakes. The smell alone made you want to eat the wax. Anyway, Dr. Goldie, a great doctor but a delusional woman with a God-complex asked him out on a date. Barrington told Dr. Goldie that he was happily married and was not interested in a relationship with her. She refused to take no for an answer. She aggressively pursued him, bought him expensive gifts which he declined, and eventually began to stalk him. The poor man stopped coming to our facility because of her. To make a long story short, she broke into his house and his young son found her sleeping in his bed. Barrington's wife was furious. Barrington called the police and had Dr. Goldie dragged out of their home. After a few more break ins, arrests, and restraining orders, the doctor ended up here among her previous patients."

"That's kinda sad," the intern sighed.

"They always say the best psychiatrists are the craziest."

Xoe the Unexpected

(Written for Sorghum & Spear: A Way of
Silk)

Xoe opens her eyes and closes them
quickly, blinded by the callous light of
sunbeams streaming through cracks in her
earthen prison. A staggering bug crawls across
her elbow. She tries to move her arm to no avail,
she's enclosed too tight, and resorts to blowing
the insect off after three angry huffs. Aching and
bruised, she bumps her head on something hard
and unforgiving. It feels like a death blow, yet
she is not that lucky. The pain swells and
swallows itself quickly. She winces and pats the
top of her head knocking grains of dirt from her
brown cottony hair into her eyes. A curse word
escapes her lips as she blinks her eyes free of
dirt.

Slowly she opens her eyes again to
survey her surroundings. Brown earth encloses
her balled up body in every direction. Chin to
knees, she tries to turn towards the light, small
rocks pressing into her delicate obsidian skin.
She manages to lift her arm enough to insert her
fingers into a jagged crack and begin to claw;
claw like badger blood flowed through her
veins, like the tips of her fingers were
indestructible. The small hole expands easily,

soil falling away in crumbly curtains. Within minutes she is able to force her head and shoulder out of the hollow like a baby breaking through the birth canal.

Her heart drums against her chest as she sees hundreds upon hundreds of Abiku milling about. Mountains with castles carved from rock tower in the background. Smoke and the smell of roasting meat scent the air along with strange spices and musky demons in every shape and size poking unidentifiable flesh turning on spits. In the center of the rocky city, there were Abiku conversing about their latest conquests, young demons sparring, and lovers holding hands in dark corners. The demons casually interact in a way that is surprising to Xoe for she always imagined them in a perpetual state of anger, growling and endlessly plotting the demise of her people. She had never imagined them as communal beings who had families and friends that they cared about. She shrugs her shoulders and dismisses her new revelation. Their seeming humanity had no bearing on her fate for she knew that their blithe interactions would change in seconds into a murderous hunt upon seeing her face.

"Hellwalk!" Xoe exclaims under her breath. Although she has never been there, legends of the foul city are widely circulated among her people. It is the land of the Abiku; the dwelling place of demons; the unholy abyss. Seeing it firsthand is both a wonder and a horror. How she came to be in such a place confuses her.

Memories of her walking with her sisters, fellowshipping after a light feast in the park and an intense session of magic lessons, then being bombarded by hooded strangers breaking through the nearby trees. Xoe remembers running from a hoard of frenzied Abiku, thirsty for her innate power; hungry for her magic, through the Pendulum Plains; being separated from her shrieking sisters and hearing their screams as they were torn apart and carried away in every direction by monsters as wicked as they are ancient. Taken by monsters that ached to steal the girls' magic and manufacture it for themselves.

The feeling of calloused hands, clawed and painful, taking hold of Xoe from behind, fear bubbling up deep within her belly and spreading like bugs when exposed to light, and then blackness is her last memory before opening her eyes in the hole in the ground that hugged her limbs like a jealous lover. Now she is in the belly of the beast alone and trapped. She instantly regrets not heeding her grandmother's warning not to go too far away from camp. Xoe and her sisters didn't listen. They never listened. Nothing ever happened to them when they explored the Pendulum Plains. They knew the danger of the plains, but they were curious about learning a new kind of magic. A magic only Dembe mastered. The political prisoner had escaped her chains and was hiding in a cave when Xoe and her sisters stumbled upon her. In return for not turning her in, Dembe agreed to teach the girls Orishian Vodun which is not powered by the lifeseed and not dictated by twilight essence. The girls were enamored by the idea of a power source that was not tied into the Namazzi bloodline.

Xoe retreats into the hole and digs until the opening is wide enough for her to escape. Pushing from the earth like a babe from the womb, Xoe slides from her earthen prison and lands roughly on the rocky ground; dust coating her pitch-colored skin in an ashy beige. She spots a nest of bushes a few feet away and instantly decides that they are her destination.

Two battle worn Abiku walk past her hollow, dragging two unconscious girls behind them. Xoe gasps at the sight of her sisters as the rocks pull bits of their flesh from their bones as they are dragged along. Withered and leathered, all magic has been drained from their bodies. The demons toss them onto a pile of wood and light it on fire.

Tears stream from Xoe's eyes. There is one sister left and Xoe had no idea where they were holding her. Xoe knew that they would be coming for them both soon.

The two Abiku move to the opposite side of the pyre and disappear behind the door of a stone carved building. Xoe cannot read the words over the door because they are written in the Abiku symbols. The sound of more Abiku heading her way is heard in the distance. She realizes that it was now or never. She bolts from the hole and runs as fast as she can across the dusty road. She whispers a small spell to erase her footprints from the dirt as she moves. The prints disappear in whiffs of dust and settle down smoothly on the ground.

After safely seeking refuge in the shrubbery, she looks around to see if there are any more holes holding captive An'fre or any other poor soul kidnapped by the demons. All other surrounding pits are empty. Traces of inhabitants litter a dozen holes with matchless shoes, torn cloth, and abandoned weapons.

Xoe peers through the brush plotting her next move. Demons are everywhere! Literally everywhere.

A crowd of demons in the center of the square begin to clap and cheer. Xoe moves behind a closer shrub to see what the commotion is all about.

The crowd parted and allowed a tall, helmeted demon to walk through. His armor brandished the most battle scars. His gnarled hands were wrapped tightly around two scimitars glistening in the sunlight. Behind him, four less decorated Abiku followed dragging the body of Xoe's sister Makuba.

Makuba, clothes torn, and body bruised, struggled against her captors. Curses and spells poured from her lips causing lesions to appear upon the skin of the demons who held her. A demon plugged her mouth with a filthy piece of cloth he tore from the hem of her garment.

Xoe clamped her hand over her mouth to prevent herself from vomiting. Burning tears blurred her vision as she watched her sister, bound and chained, being led to a makeshift podium amid a hoard of demons.

The tall demon rambled something in his native tongue that caused the surrounding Abiku to go into a joyous uproar. Howling and laughing Abiku voices bounced off the mountains in an endless wave of echoes. Makuba fruitlessly pulled at her restraints as the tall demon finished his speech and attached her wrist chains to a pole with a high hook.

Makuba spit into the eye of the tall demon. He wiped the spittle away with the back of his hand and let out a thundering belly laugh.

Xoe fell back on her behind trying to force herself to think of a strategy to save her sister. If Makuba, her strongest sister, cannot free herself, what can Xoe do? Her palms beat upon her head like a tambourine. Broken spells swam through her head. She could never remember spells. It usually took her weeks to memorize her spell work. She was not like her other sisters. Magic was not a passion for Xoe. Her powers were weak in comparison to those closer to the bloodline of Eshe.

Xoe only did magic because she was expected to, not because she wanted to. The voice of her grandmother telling her that she was more powerful than she imagined and to study and practice echoed through her head. Her grandmother told her stories of how her mother was so filled with twilight that it glowed from her fingertips and eyes when it was dark. She claimed that Xoe glowed too. Xoe didn't believe this because her spell work rarely worked, and she was usually the butt of her sister's jokes, so Xoe simply stopped focusing on magic. She couldn't count how many times she pretended to work on her magic when she was simply composing a song or thinking about the next time she and her sisters could escape to see Dembe.

Dembe's independence was Xoe's dream. Dembe's magic is the magic Xoe desired, a magic that was free from tradition and the eyes of the elders. Now all she had to do was to remember the last spell Dembe had taught.

A roar comes from the crowd of demons again as a hooded figure walks through the crowd and approaches the podium. Every instinct in Xoe's being tells her that the creature was there to harness her sister's magic. It wants to suck out her twilight so they can gain enough power to take the lifeseed for themselves. The cloaked creature moves with the rhythm of a serpent; its yellow eyes like flames of fire, its claws holding a pulsating orb like a blue moon.

Makuba spit the cloth to the ground and uttered a spell. The org falls from the creature's hand and rolls across the ground through the feet of the demons. The tall demon backhand slaps Makuba. Blood spatters across the front of her shirt as the demons scrambled to grab the rolling org. The hooded creature stood patiently waiting for its orb.

Xoe lifts her head above the shrubs. Mukuba's eyes locks with hers. Hope replaces the desperation in Mukuba's eyes. She smiles.

The hooded creature lifts its ancient face upward and begins to sniff like it smells the shift from fear to faith. It turns to Makuba and follows her gaze to Xoe. The hooded creature points its leathery fingers and the heads of the Abiku turn towards Xoe. They grab the swords from their sheaths and wait for a signal from their leader to attack.

Xoe steps from behind the shrubs onto the open road. She prays silently to her ancestors to help her. She begs the women who had gone before her to imbue her with their power. Xoe channels the voice of her grandmother and locks onto the memory of every story she ever told. Xoe plants her feet deep into the earth and raises her arms high in the air. She inhales slowly and exhales. If there is twilight in her veins, it must present itself now. If Dembe's magic is real, it must join with Xoe's twilight to save her sister.

Xoe's lips part. Nothing happens. Her hands tremble as tears stream down her face. Makuba's trusting eyes marries Xoe's letting her know that every confidence is in her. Xoe opens her mouth again to call upon her ancestors. A tingling feeling crawls from the soles of her feet to the crown of her head. Words pour from her mouth in uncontrollable waves; words that she has never uttered. Words she has never heard. Her body quakes like a woman possessed as spells ring against the mountains of Hellwalk. Dark clouds form overhead. Lightning strikes the four corners of the square. The whites of Xoe's eyes shine a bright blue, so does her onyx fingertips.

The Abiku scatter; all except the tall one and the cloaked creature.

Makuba's eyes stretch in bewilderment as her sister's bare feet lift from the earth. Xoe levitates a few feet from the ground, head falling backwards as her thundering voice cause the surrounding buildings to quake. The hooded creature pulls back its hood to reveal an ancient feminine face, skeletal and demonic.

The creature lifts its hand as Xoe points her palm at the beast. Bright blue light shoots from Xoe's hand and knocks the creature from its podium. The tall Abiku scrambles to the ancient creature's side.

Xoe's feet touch the ground, and she runs to her sister. With a strength unknown, Xoe breaks Makuba's chains and frees her. The two run into a nearby cave and embrace.

"How did you do that?" Makuba asks, her body frail and weak with hunger and deprivation.

"I don't know," Xoe admits. "How do we get out of here?"

Makuba grabs Xoe's hands and asks her to join in a chant. After minutes of repetitive words, the two fade away and reappear on the outskirts of their village. A woman weaving a basket looks up and sees the two girls in her front yard. She recognizes them immediately. She drops her basket and runs to wrap her arms around her daughters.

Questions for Book Clubs

1. What are some of the reoccurring themes in the stories?
2. Which was your favorite story? Why?
3. Which is your least favorite story? Why?
4. Who was the most likable/dislikable character(s)? Why?
5. How did the stories make you feel?
6. Were the plots engaging?
7. If you could ask the author a question, what would you ask?
8. Did you learn anything new?
9. Were the stories predictable?
10. Were there any plot twists that surprised you?

Violette L. Meier is a happily married mother, writer, folk artist, poet, inspirational leader and native of Atlanta, Georgia, who earned her B.A. in English at Clark Atlanta University and a Master of Divinity at Interdenominational Theological Center.

The great-granddaughter of a dream interpreter, Violette is a lover of all things supernatural and enjoys writing paranormal, fantasy, and horror among other speculative fiction genres. She is the author of fourteen books and is always working on something new.

To learn more about Violette, please visit her at VioletteMeier.com.